Mary-Kate Olsen   Ashley Olsen

so little time

D1512050

Check out these other great
so little time
titles:

Mary-Kate Olsen   Ashley Olsen

so little time

how to train a boy

By Jacqueline Carrol

Based on the teleplay by Eric Cohen & Tonya Hurley

HarperEntertainment
An Imprint of HarperCollins*Publishers*
A PARACHUTE PRESS BOOK

A PARACHUTE PRESS BOOK

Parachute Publishing, L.L.C.
156 Fifth Avenue, Suite 302
New York, NY 10010

Published by
HarperEntertainment
An *Imprint of* HarperCollins*Publishers*
10 East 53rd Street, New York, NY 10022-5299

ISBN 0-06-008368-9

HarperCollins®, ☰®, and HarperEntertainment™ are trademarks of HarperCollins Publishers Inc.

First printing: January 2002

Printed in the United States of America

Visit HarperEntertainment on the World Wide Web at
www.harpercollins.com

10 9 8 7 6 5 4 3 2 1

chapter
one

"**H**urry up, Riley!" fourteen-year-old Chloe Carlson called to her sister. "I need to do my hair."

"I'll be out in a second!" Riley called back from the bathroom.

Chloe kept staring intently out the window of the bedroom she shared with Riley. Left was the street. Right was the beach. She gave each view a three-second scan. Pavement on the left. Sand on the right.

Nobody in sight.

The bathroom door opened, and Chloe's sister came into the bedroom. Riley's shoulder-length blond hair was wet from the shower. Chloe's longer blond hair was covered with soft curlers.

"Here I am," Riley announced, wrapping a towel around her head. "How's the boywatch going?"

"No one so far," Chloe replied. She'd come up with the idea of a before-school boywatch last week, on the first day of school. That was the first time she'd ever seen Travis Morgan.

She'd been standing in the exact same place when she spotted him down on the beach. She didn't know his name then, of course. But she thought he looked really cute. Short brown hair, long tan legs. She'd watched as he climbed the stairs to the street and disappeared from sight.

Then, that same day, she'd seen him at West Malibu High, where she and Riley had just started as freshmen. And he wasn't just cute, he was hot.

Thanks to her friend Tara Jordan's older brother, Chloe now knew Travis's name. She also knew he was a junior, and that he didn't have a girlfriend (yet). What she didn't know was Travis himself.

"He has to walk by again *sometime*," she murmured, still staring out the window.

"Sure he does," Riley agreed. "Didn't Tara's brother say he was having trouble with his dirt bike?"

Chloe nodded. That was another thing she'd learned about Travis—he had a dirt bike, and he hung out with some other guys who had them, too. They all had a reputation for cutting classes and getting detention.

[Chloe: I know, I know. You're thinking, "Stay away from this guy, Chloe. Detention, dirt bikes...definitely bad news." But you wouldn't be saying that if you'd met Travis. Okay, well, I haven't exactly met him, either, but there's no way a boy that cute could be bad news. I'm telling you, I know about these things. Or at least I'm willing to find out.]

Chloe crossed her fingers, hoping that Travis would have major trouble with his bike. Then when he walked by again, she could "bump" into him.

"If I can just get a chance to talk to him, I'm sure I can make him like me," she said to Riley. "I've passed him in the hall three times this week, but he hardly notices me."

"Probably because you're a freshman," Riley said, taking some clothes out of the closet. "It's like we're marked."

"I know," Chloe agreed. "That's why I need to get into a conversation with him. Today I'm going to try to find out where his locker is."

"Then what?" Riley asked.

"I'll play lost and ask directions to the science wing or someplace."

"Bad idea," Riley advised. "I mean, this is Friday, right? We started school last Wednesday. If you don't know where the science wing is by now, Travis will think you're totally clueless."

"Good point," Chloe agreed, trying to think of something else she could ask Travis.

Riley finished changing into jeans and a peach-colored top. "Okay, my turn at the window."

As soon as Riley took her place, Chloe hurried to the dresser across the room. "At least the boywatch isn't a total loss," Chloe said, taking the rollers from her hair. "I haven't seen Larry, either."

"You mean you haven't seen him *yet*," Riley told her.

"True," Chloe admitted. Larry Slotnick, their next-door neighbor, almost always managed to show up. He'd had a crush on Riley since first grade, and no matter how many times Riley turned him down, he still kept asking her out.

"I've been thinking," Chloe said as she brushed her hair. "You know what your problem is, Riley?"

[**Riley**: Okay, here's the thing—even though Chloe and I are both fourteen, she was born eight minutes earlier. That makes her my "older" sister, so she likes giving me advice.]

"What's my problem?" Riley asked. She picked up the towel and began briskly rubbing her hair. She wore hers straight and didn't need quite as much mirror time.

"Well, for one thing, you shouldn't dry your hair like that," Chloe said. "It'll get all snarled and then you'll have split ends."

"That's my problem—split ends?" Riley asked.

"It will be if you're not careful." Chloe opened her jewelry box and took out a pair of blue enameled earrings to go with the blue top she was wearing. "You're supposed to just squeeze your hair with the towel."

Riley started squeezing her hair.

"Your other problem is boys," Chloe said, putting the earrings in her ears. "You're way too picky."

Riley stared at her.

"Keep watching out the window!" Chloe cried. "It takes only fifteen seconds for somebody to walk by. I timed it."

"Wait—back up to my problem with boys," Riley said, turning to the window again. "Don't tell me you think I should go out with Larry."

"Well, no," Chloe admitted.

"Good." Riley breathed a sigh of relief. "Because I like Larry, but not that way. He's a friend—a very goofy friend. We've known him forever, remember?"

"Yes, but forget about Larry," Chloe said. "The problem is, you're always getting crushes on actors and rock stars. They seem perfect and you know why? Because they're not real."

"They're not?" Riley asked. "Whoa, has anybody told them? Does Brad Pitt know he's not real?"

Chloe laughed. "You know what I mean. They're fantasy guys. Real boys have rough edges. You sort of have to mold them. But at least you have a chance with them."

"Like you have with Travis, you mean."

"Exactly," Chloe agreed. "Just because Travis hasn't noticed me yet doesn't mean he never will. Travis is *possible*, see? I just have to find a way to make it happen."

Checking her hair again, Chloe tried to think of other ways to make it happen with Travis. Once she learned where his locker was, she and her friends could hang out around there before homeroom. Maybe she'd try to find out his class schedule, too, so she'd have maximum opportunities to meet him.

A rap on the door interrupted Chloe's thoughts. She glanced up as her mother hurried into the room.

Macy Carlson was slender, with brown hair and eyes and a habit of speaking quickly, especially when she was nervous or under pressure. "What do you think?" she asked, holding out an armful of filmy material dotted with tiny jet beads and rhinestones.

"It's gorgeous. Is that for the MTV dress?" Chloe asked. The MTV awards would be broadcast in less than two weeks, and their mother had been hired to design a dress for a model named Tedi. Tedi was going to present an award. That meant Mom's dress would be seen by millions of people. Needless to say, it was a big deal.

Mrs. Carlson nodded. "It's going to be ankle-length, and I'm thinking scalloped hemline, maybe higher in front, but not knee-high, that would be too Flamenco dancer, I just want a nice swirly effect so the beads and rhinestones will catch the light," she said without taking a breath.

"Slow down, Mom," Riley told her.

"And calm down," Chloe added.

"Not possible," Macy said. "This is the first dress I've

designed on my own since your dad left the business, and it has to be an absolute knockout." She rushed out the door, then popped her head back in. "See you two later. Love you!"

"Love you, too, Mom," Chloe called. She turned to Riley. "Mom's really hyper today."

"She's always been hyper," Riley said as their mother's footsteps clattered down the hall. "Now she's practically a wreck."

"Um-hmm," Chloe agreed, applying some lip gloss. It had been several months since their parents decided to have a "trial separation." Before that, they'd run a fashion-design business together. Now their mother was running it on her own. Chloe knew she could do it, but it was sort of like living with a whirlwind.

Their dad, on the other hand, was so calm, he was almost asleep. He hadn't taken another job yet, but he wasn't worried since he had plenty of investments. He'd just bought a house trailer to live in on a bluff overlooking the beach.

"What do you think Dad's new place will be like?" Chloe asked. She and Riley were going to see it for the first time today after school.

Riley turned to face Chloe. "When I talked to him yesterday, he said it's perfect for him," Riley replied. "Small and simple. That's what he wanted, remember? A simpler life."

"I guess you can't get much simpler than a single-wide trailer," Chloe agreed. As she leaned toward the mirror for a final inspection, she saw a face pop up in the window—spiky brown hair, close-together eyes, a big mouth, and a goofy, hopeful expression.

Larry Slotnick's face.

Larry's head stayed visible for approximately two seconds, then disappeared.

"Riley," Chloe said.

"I saw him. Did you leave the trampoline out again?" Riley asked accusingly.

"Oops." Chloe grinned. "Sorry. Ignore him. Maybe he'll go away."

"It's Larry," Riley reminded her. "He never goes away."

Larry's face bounced back into the window frame. "Riley!" he called. "Will you…" He disappeared again.

Riley hung her towel over the closet doorknob and joined Chloe at the dresser.

Larry bounced into view. "Riley, will you go out with me?" he asked quickly.

"No." Riley began combing her still-damp hair.

Larry disappeared and bounced up again. This time he grabbed hold of the window ledge and clung to it. "Give me one good reason why not," he said.

Riley glanced at his reflection in the mirror. "Because you're hanging from my window?" she asked with a grin.

"Okay, you have a point," Larry agreed. "But, Riley, I

can't help myself. You're the only thing in the world I need to be happy. Just you."

Chloe turned around. "That's it?" she asked him. "Just Riley?"

Larry thought for a second. "Well, and maybe my PlayStation Two. But that's it," he added quickly. "Just Riley and my PlayStation Two. That's all I'll ever need." He paused. "And maybe a breakfast burrito."

Riley couldn't help laughing as she crossed the room and picked up her backpack.

"So is it okay if I hang for a while?" Larry asked. "Just make believe I'm not here."

Riley slung her pack over her shoulder, gave Chloe and Larry a little wave, and headed out the door.

Chloe walked over to the window. She couldn't help feeling a little sympathy for Larry. After all, they were both trying to attract someone.

Of course, that was absolutely all they had in common. As she'd told Riley, Travis was possible. She had a chance with him. But for Larry, Riley was definitely not possible.

"Hey, Chloe, do you think Riley's coming back?" Larry asked.

"I guess she'll have to, eventually." Chloe took one more glance out the window and gasped.

"What?" Startled, Larry tightened his grip on the window ledge. "What's wrong?"

"Nothing. Just slide over—quick!" Chloe told him.

She had just spotted a boy in the distance, walking along the beach. Was it Travis?

"Actually, I think I'll just hop down and head to school," Larry said.

As Larry dropped down to the trampoline, Chloe peered out the window at the boy. He was farther away than when Chloe had seen him last week. She squinted, trying to bring him into focus.

Jeans and a black T-shirt. Brown hair? Yes, definitely. But was it him?

The guy still wasn't close enough for her to see any more details. But Chloe wasn't waiting any longer. She grabbed her bookbag and rushed from the room. If it *was* Travis, this could be her big chance!

chapter
two

Trotting down the stairs, Riley wondered how long Larry would actually hang from the window. This whole thing with him was almost like a game—for Riley, anyway. But even though Larry joked about it, too, he really did want her to go out with him.

One of these days she'd have to figure out a way to make him give up. She'd have to be firm but nice, because she didn't want to lose him as a friend. But anything more just wasn't going to happen between them.

When Riley walked into the kitchen, Manuelo was at the stove, stirring something in a saucepan.

Tall and dark-haired, with a wicked sense of humor, Manuelo had been the Carlsons' cook/housekeeper for fourteen years. He didn't just cook and clean, though. He helped Riley and Chloe with their homework, traded jokes with them, and taught them how to play pool.

Since Manuelo was practically a member of the

family by now, he didn't bother to hide his moods. And from the way he was whipping that spoon around, Riley could tell he wasn't happy about something.

"What's the matter?" she asked him.

Manuelo sighed dramatically. "Your mother needs to do a preliminary fitting of that MTV dress, and the model hasn't shown up yet," he reported.

"Uh-oh. Mom freaked out, didn't she?" Riley asked.

"She started to," Manuelo said. "But then she found a stand-in."

"Who?"

"Guess." Holding a big spoon, Manuelo turned from the stove and struck a model's pose.

"Stunning." Riley grinned and pointed to the spoon. "I especially like the dripping oatmeal."

Manuelo quickly stuck the spoon back in the saucepan before the oatmeal plopped to the floor. "Where's your sister?" he asked. "This stuff can turn into a brick in seconds."

"I'm sure she'll be here soon," Riley said. "I left her upstairs with Larry."

Manuelo peered at her over his shoulder, surprised. "Larry's upstairs?"

"Yeah, he sort of popped by to hang a while." Riley explained the situation. "Anyway, Chloe was hoping she'd see Travis Morgan again, but so far he's a no-show."

Riley poured herself some orange juice, took a bowl

of oatmeal from Manuelo, and slid into a chair. As she dipped her spoon into the cereal, Chloe rushed into the kitchen.

"Did you see him?" Chloe demanded breathlessly. She ran to the window. "Is he up to the house yet?"

"Who? Travis?" Riley asked. "You mean he's really out there?"

"I saw…" As Chloe gazed out the window, her shoulders suddenly slumped. "No. It's not him."

Riley peered around her sister just in time to see a man in jeans and a black T-shirt walk past on the beach. He had brown hair, but he was at least thirty years old.

"Too bad, Chloe," Riley said. "But you'll still see Travis at school." Her stomach growled. She pulled her spoon from the cereal bowl and the entire contents came with it.

"What is *that*?" Chloe asked, pointing to the bowl-shaped lump of oatmeal.

"Breakfast," Manuelo told her. He peered into the saucepan. "Sit down and I'll hack off a piece for you."

"Uh, I think I'll skip." Chloe placed her backpack on an empty chair and looked out the window again.

Manuelo dumped the hardened oatmeal in the trash and began packing their lunch bags.

Chloe glanced over her shoulder. "Manuelo, that's not an apple you're putting in my lunch, is it?" she asked.

"Wait, let me check." Manuelo took a bite of the

apple and chewed it thoughtfully. "Yes. Macintosh, I believe."

"I can't eat an apple in school," Chloe told him. "No one looks good eating an apple. Pieces get stuck between your teeth. Juice runs down your chin. Plus it's loud. You've got to chomp it like a horse."

Manuelo glanced at Riley. "Do you understand this?"

Riley laughed. "Chloe has this theory that in front of boys, you eat only *cute* food."

Manuelo frowned. "'Cute food?'"

Chloe nodded. "Like grapes. Seedless, of course." Walking to the counter, she peered into one of the paper sacks, then pulled out a small plastic bag. "Celery *and* carrot sticks? Way too noisy."

Riley gave Manuelo a fake frown. "Are you trying to destroy her? Think *cute.*"

"Ah-ha." Manuelo opened the refrigerator and pulled out a head of cabbage. He took a Magic Marker from the junk drawer, and quickly drew a happy face on the cabbage. "How's this?" he asked with a wicked grin. "Is this cute enough?"

Riley laughed. Chloe rolled her eyes. Still grinning, Manuelo strode to the door, tossing the cabbage to Chloe on his way out of the kitchen.

"Nobody takes me seriously," Chloe grumbled. She returned the smiling cabbage to the refrigerator and took out a can of Coke.

"Sure we do," Riley said. "Except when you're talking about something ridiculous, like cute food."

The phone rang and Chloe grabbed it. "Hello? Oh, hi. Hang on." She held the phone out to Riley. "It's Sierra."

Sierra Pomeroy was Riley's best friend. Her real name was Sarah, but only her parents and teachers called her that. In fact, they didn't have a clue that she used another name at school.

The Pomeroys were nice but kind of old-fashioned. They didn't believe in phone calls before nine in the morning or after ten at night unless it was an emergency. Since it was only eight-fifteen, Riley figured something major was up. She hurried to the counter and took the phone.

"Riley!" Sierra's voice crackled with excitement. "You'll never guess what happened! The Wave got its first gig!"

"You're kidding!" Riley gasped.

The Wave was a rock band Sierra and some friends had formed back in seventh grade. Her parents were clueless about the band, too. As far as they were concerned, their daughter was a quiet girl who played first violin in the school orchestra.

All true—except the quiet part. *Sarah* was quiet. *Sierra* was a throaty-voiced, hip-wiggling bass guitarist. Sierra's parents didn't know anything about her double life, and all her friends had sworn to keep it a secret.

"Sierra, that's fantastic!" Riley said.

"What happened? What's going on?" Chloe asked.

Riley quickly told her.

"Way to go, Sierra!" Sitting at the table, Chloe raised her Coke can in a toast.

"Where's the gig?" Riley asked Sierra.

"California Dream!" Sierra squealed.

"You're kidding," Riley said again. California Dream was a local beach club and hangout. "This is so great!"

"I know, I can't believe it," Sierra agreed. "And all I need is…" She suddenly lowered her voice. "Gotta go, Mom's coming. But I need your help. Talk to you at school, okay?"

"Okay. Bye." Riley hung up and turned to Chloe. "Is that fantastic or what?"

Chloe didn't respond. Clutching the can of ice-cold Coke, she gazed toward the window with an agonized expression on her face.

Uh-oh, Riley thought. Brain freeze.

Every time Chloe ate or drank something cold, her sinuses seized up and she could barely function until the pain went away.

"Taah!" Pinching the bridge of her noise, Chloe moaned and gestured helplessly with her free hand.

"Hang on, Chloe," Riley said soothingly. "I know it hurts, but it doesn't last long. What's the record? A minute?"

"Teraahh!" Chloe moaned more loudly and tried to stand up. "Teraahh!"

Teraahh? What was that supposed to mean? Riley thought a second. Then she finally got it. "Travis?" she cried. "He's out there?"

Chloe managed to nod.

Riley sped around the table and looked out the window. Sure enough, Travis Morgan was walking up the beach, getting closer with every step. He was barefoot, with his sneakers tied together and slung over his shoulder with his backpack.

Now he was close enough for Riley to see the glint of the tiny gold piercing in his ear, and the way the sun had bleached his eyebrows until they were almost white.

No wonder Chloe wants to get to know him, she thought. He is definitely hot.

As Travis walked out of sight, Chloe's brain freeze finally ended. "I can't believe it." She groaned. "He finally shows up and I'm paralyzed!"

"Well, come on!" Riley grabbed her backpack. "He just walked by. There's still time to catch him."

"Are you kidding? I'm not going to chase after him," Chloe said. She thought a second, then jumped up. "Of course, it's time to go to school, anyway. And if we just happen to catch up to him…"

"Right," Riley agreed. "Let's go!"

chapter
three

"There he is!" Chloe said as she and Riley hurried outside. She pointed to Travis, who'd left the beach and was walking down the street.

"You go ahead," Riley told her. "Three's a crowd, right? Good luck."

"Thanks!" Travis had a good head start, so Chloe began to run. Not the coolest thing to do, she thought, but she'd worry about that after she caught up with him.

She could tell him she liked to stay in shape and always jogged to school. Or that she was going out for the track team.

Travis was almost at the corner. Chloe ran faster. Her bookbag slammed against her back and she could practically hear her hair starting to frizz. Her legs felt rubbery. Maybe she *should* start a jogging program.

A piece of paper fluttered across the street in front

of her. Inspiration hit. As Travis turned the corner, Chloe slowed and snatched up the paper.

"Hey, wait up, you dropped something!" she shouted, waving the paper in the air. She didn't look at it, so she didn't know if it was actually his, but that didn't matter. It was a perfect excuse to start a conversation.

She sped around the corner, expecting to see Travis up ahead. "You dropped—" she started to yell. Then she stopped, breathless.

Travis was up ahead, all right. But so was one of his friends, Kyle something or other. And Kyle was on his dirt bike, which was making way too much noise for Chloe to yell over.

Stuffing the piece of paper into her bookbag, Chloe watched as Travis climbed onto the bike behind Kyle. Kyle revved the motor, turned the bike in a wide circle, then roared back down the street toward Chloe.

As the bike sped by, Travis glanced at Chloe for about a tenth of a second.

> [Chloe: Did you get that? He actually looked at me. This is good. I mean, I don't exactly look my best at the moment. But he did see me. Our eyes met. And next time, he'll remember me. Mark my words. This-boy-will-remember-me.]

As soon as Riley entered West Malibu High, she hurried into the girls' bathroom in the music wing and glanced around. The stalls were empty. Carrie Thompson and Joelle Myers were at the mirrors, brushing their hair.

"Have you seen Sierra?" Riley asked. Sierra always began the day in the girls' room. That's where she would change from the Sarah clothes she left her house in to the Sierra clothes she wore until she went back home.

Joelle shook her head and held up a hand. "Listen."

Riley listened. Off-key strains of "The Blue Danube" floated through the wall. The orchestra was practicing.

Oh, right, Riley remembered. Sierra had an early practice with the band.

"Hey, Saul Bertram told me that The Wave is playing at California Dream," Carrie said to Riley.

Riley nodded. Saul was the Wave's drummer. "Isn't it great?"

"Awesome," Carrie agreed. "Do you think Sierra's parents will find out?"

"Let's hope not," Riley said.

The door banged open and Sierra rushed in, carrying her violin case and bookbag. She was tall and thin, with wavy red hair pulled back in a neat ponytail. "How much time do I have?" she asked breathlessly.

Riley checked her watch. "Four minutes."

Sierra dropped her bookbag and set the violin down. "Okay, I can do this," she said, unzipping her tan knee-length skirt.

Sierra's double life had turned her into a quick-change artist. She kept a couple of cool tops and pairs of jeans in her locker and switched into them at school.

Joelle and Carrie headed for the door. "Hey, congratulations on California Dream," Joelle said to Sierra.

"Yeah, we'll be there for sure," Carrie told her.

"Thanks!" Sierra said. As the door swung shut she stepped out of her skirt. "I'm still floating!" she said to Riley. "California Dream—can you believe it?"

"It's awesome," Riley agreed. "But the place is kind of close. I mean, aren't you afraid your parents might find out?"

"Maybe a little," Sierra admitted, toeing off her sneakers. "But they don't exactly hang out there. Plus the poster doesn't say 'The Wave and Sierra, a.k.a. Sarah Pomeroy.' It just has the name of the band."

"I guess you're right." Riley pulled a pair of low-rise jeans from Sierra's bag and held them out. "When are you playing?"

"Next Saturday night," Sierra said, struggling into the tight jeans. "Only a week from tomorrow. We're going to rehearse at Saul's house every minute we can. Of course, Mom and Dad'll think I'm busy with the orchestra or studying at the library or something. Anyway, I need your help."

"Right, that's what you told me on the phone." Riley folded Sierra's skirt and slipped it into the bookbag. "So what do you need? Something to wear?"

Sierra checked her yellow top in the mirror, then pulled the elastic from her ponytail. "I need to look really great, better than great. *Awesome*! Do you think your mom

21

would lend me one of the outfits she designed?"

Riley stared at her. "You're kidding, right? You know she treats her designs like they're made of gold. What if you tore it or something?"

"I wouldn't," Sierra insisted, shaking out her long red hair. "I'd be really, really careful."

"Sierra, I've seen you with the band," Riley argued. "You kick and jump around and practically do somersaults. If you didn't tear the outfit, you'd sweat all over it for sure."

"Please, Riley, just ask her," Sierra begged. She tugged her sneakers back on and picked up her bag and violin. "I mean, this is our first gig! It would be so cool if I could wear an actual designer outfit."

"It would," Riley agreed. "Okay, I guess I can ask."

"Thanks, Riley!" Sierra grinned as they headed out the door. "See you at lunch!"

"Right." As Riley hurried down the hall toward homeroom, she tried to figure out a good time to ask her mother about borrowing an outfit. Mom would have to be calm. Wait, she was never calm. Okay, semi-calm. Maybe when she was taking a bubble bath.

Except she never took bubble baths when she was in the middle of a design. Only showers.

She liked to watch reruns on the Comedy Channel. Of course, she did that only if a design was going well. If it wasn't, she watched old sad movies so she'd have a good excuse to cry.

Riley crossed her fingers, hoping the MTV design went well. Otherwise, Sierra would be totally out of luck.

Riley had almost reached her classroom when she spotted Larry at the other end of the hall.

Naturally, Larry spotted her, too. "Hi, Riley!" he called out.

"Hi, Larry."

"I have a question," Larry said when he reached her.

He looked serious, Riley thought. Was something wrong? "What?" she asked.

"Will you go out with me?" Larry's face broke into a grin. "Gotcha, huh?"

Riley rolled her eyes, but she couldn't help laughing. "That's right. You got me, Larry."

"So will you?"

"No, Larry."

"I knew you'd say that," he told her. "But I'm going to keep asking."

Shaking her head, Riley hurried into science class. There had to be a way to stop Larry from showing up and asking her out all the time. She didn't want to hurt his feelings, though.

Well, she'd come up with something. In the meantime, she reminded herself to put the trampoline away when she got home.

"Nine ninety-six?" Chloe asked her friends Tara Jordan and Quinn Reyes in the hall. "You're sure?"

Tara nodded, her dark eyes sparkling. "Positive. Quinn and I both saw him taking a book out."

"It's Travis's locker for sure," Quinn added. She nudged Chloe in the arm. "Go on, get over there."

"Right. Okay, thanks, guys." Chloe took a deep breath and walked down the hall toward locker 996. She waved to Quinn and Tara, who had to get to their next class.

Chloe had lunch now, but what was a little hunger if it meant seeing Travis Morgan?

As kids hurried by on their way to class or lunch, Chloe casually leaned against locker 996 and scanned the crowd.

No Travis yet. Of course, he might not come to his locker now, but Chloe decided to stick around anyway.

A couple of minutes went by. Still no Travis. Chloe unzipped her bookbag and took out the sheet of paper she'd picked up that morning. She had to think of something cool to say when she gave it to Travis.

Hmm, she thought. What about: "Hi, I think you dropped this." No good. "Hi, remember me? You passed me on Kyle's dirt bike this morning." Even worse. "Hi. This fell out of your backpack when you were walking down my street this morning. I thought it might be important." Better.

"Excuse me," someone said. "You're kind of in my way."

Chloe glanced up, into the gray-green eyes of Travis Morgan. "Oh! Sorry." She quickly slid over.

Travis opened his locker and shoved a book inside.

"Um…" Chloe said. "I think you…remember when…" She stopped. Get a grip, she told herself.

"Did you say something?" Travis asked. He was moving some books around and was half-hidden by the locker door.

"Yes." As Chloe smoothed out the sheet of paper, she actually looked at it for the first time. It read:

OH, BABY!

WHAT A STORE!

• CRIBS • STROLLERS • CLOTHES • TOYS • DOOR PRIZES •

GRAND OPENING SEPTEMBER 25

OH, BABY, DON'T MISS IT!

"Oh, Baby"? Oh, no! Chloe thought. It was just a stupid ad. She had seen one at her house yesterday. This one probably blew out of someone's garbage. She couldn't possibly pretend she thought Travis dropped it. He'd think she was a total idiot.

Travis slammed his locker shut and glanced at her.

Chloe crumpled the paper in her hand. "Hi," she managed to say.

"Hi." Spinning the lock, Travis turned and walked down the hall.

Chloe groaned. So much for *that* conversation.

A few minutes later, Chloe sat down in the cafeteria and glanced around. Fourth-period lunch was the absolute worst, she decided. Tara and Quinn and the rest of her friends had fifth-period lunch, so here she was, sitting alone with nobody to talk to.

A chair screeched and Chloe glanced across the table. Amanda Gray plunked her tray down and dropped her backpack on the floor.

Okay, Chloe wasn't sitting alone anymore. But she still didn't have anyone to talk to because she and Amanda weren't friends. They weren't enemies or anything, but Amanda didn't hang out with Chloe's group. She just didn't seem to fit in anywhere.

For one thing, she sort of matched her last name. Not that she always wore gray, but she just kind of faded into the background wherever she was. She never hung out with anybody. And she was so shy, she hardly even talked.

Amanda gave Chloe a quick smile as she sat down. Chloe smiled back. Amanda immediately dropped her eyes to her tray of meat loaf and mashed potatoes.

Chloe took a big bite of her chocolate-frosted doughnut. She figured she deserved it. No breakfast, and she'd forgotten to repack a lunch. Plus she'd had two chances with Travis and blown them both. She took another bite and glanced across the table again.

Amanda's head was still down, as if she found the meat loaf incredibly fascinating. Chloe watched her thoughtfully.

Amanda had really nice hair. The ends were a mess,

but it was a nice shiny brown. And her brown eyes sparkled. Of course, you could hardly see her eyes, the way her hair hung in them.

In her mind, Chloe lopped off about three inches of Amanda's hair. Not enough. Another two inches vanished.

By the time Chloe was finished, Amanda's hair was in a smooth, chin-length bob. Much better. Chloe added a sparkly hair-slide, smoky eye shadow, and put some blusher on the girl's cheeks. She replaced the way-too-pale blue top with a cranberry-red one.

Incredible, Chloe thought as she stared at her creation. Amanda is actually pretty. Or she could be. And if she'd open her mouth and talk once in a while, she could probably be popular, too.

Chloe wondered if she should clue Amanda in. She bit off another chunk of doughnut and decided she should. After all, everybody wanted to look good and be popular, didn't they?

Chloe swallowed and cleared her throat. "Hey, Amanda?"

Amanda looked up, her forkful of potatoes halfway to her mouth. She waited expectantly.

"Did you ever think of..." But Chloe didn't finish the question. Her eyes were suddenly riveted on the doorway of the cafeteria.

And on Travis Morgan, who was just walking in with his friend Kyle.

Chloe hadn't seen Travis in fourth-period lunch

before. Maybe he'd switched. Anyway, who cared? He was here!

Chloe watched, heart thumping, as Travis and Kyle bought sandwiches and drinks, then began threading their way through the tables. There wasn't much room at any table except hers. Oh, God. Maybe they'll sit here! Chloe thought. Her heart thumped faster.

Kyle waved to somebody. Chloe quickly glanced over her shoulder. Two dirt-biker friends were out on the low wall surrounding the quad, waving back through the big glass window.

They weren't going to sit inside. But Chloe couldn't let this chance go by. Kyle was slightly ahead of Travis. As soon as he passed, she scooted her chair back with a loud screech. The sound caught Travis's attention, just as she knew it would. He turned his head.

Chloe sent him her best smile. She knew it was her best because she'd practiced it in front of the mirror— lips apart, teeth gleaming, eyes sparkling.

Travis stared. He actually stopped for a split second and stared. But then he quickly shifted his gaze away and walked on by.

What was that all about? Chloe wondered. Okay, so he didn't stop to talk, but what was that weird expression on his face? All she did was smile at him.

Confused, Chloe glanced across the table. Amanda was looking at her, silently tapping a finger against her front teeth.

Huh? Chloe whipped her compact out of her back-pack and smiled into the little mirror. "Oh, no!" She groaned.

Chocolate frosting clung to every one of her front teeth. She looked toothless and totally disgusting, like somebody who'd never gone to a dentist in her life!

Chloe ran her tongue across her teeth and glanced at Amanda again. Amanda had gone back to eating mashed potatoes.

Which is exactly what I should have eaten, Chloe thought miserably. At least they're the right color.

She glanced out at the quad, where Travis was sitting with his friends. They were definitely cool-looking, and Chloe was obviously not the only one who thought so. Every girl out there kept glancing at them.

From now on, I eat outside, Chloe thought. Maybe I'll even read up on dirt bikes so I'll have something to say when I finally get a chance to talk to him.

But first, I'll floss.

chapter
four

"It was horrible," Chloe told Riley as they walked to their father's trailer park after school. "You should have seen my teeth. I just couldn't believe it. It was totally embarrassing."

Riley couldn't believe it, either. When it came to the way she looked, Chloe almost never made a mistake. "What happened to eating cute food?" she asked.

"I know—I goofed," Chloe admitted. "I was starving and those doughnuts looked so good. I never expected to see Travis at lunch. But I'll be ready from now on."

"But are you ready for this?" Riley gestured toward the trailer park their father had just moved to. Its name was Vista del Mar. Everybody called it Vista del Car.

[Riley: So why is our dad living in a trailer park, when Chloe, Mom, and I are in a beautiful Malibu beach house? Good question. Maybe it's part of the reason why Mom and Dad broke up in the first place. **Mom is really driven. You know, power suits, power lunches, power workouts. And Dad, well, he's into yoga and meditation and lowering your cholesterol through acupuncture and all that. Total opposites. Totally fighting all the time. Dad said he just wanted to get back to basics. It was a little weird when they first separated, but now Chloe and I agree that it was probably for the best. We see Dad all the time. And now that they're not living together, Mom and Dad get along pretty well.]**

"Which one is Dad's trailer?" Chloe asked.

"Well, he said it was the smallest one." Riley glanced around. All the trailers were big except for a brown and white one about ten feet wide. "I guess that's it," she said, pointing.

"It's tiny!" Chloe exclaimed.

"Dad called it compact," Riley told her.

"Same thing," Chloe said.

As Riley and Chloe approached the trailer, the door opened and their father stepped onto its small wooden deck.

Jake Carlson wore shorts, flip-flops, and a baseball cap on his brown hair. "Hi, you two," he called, wiping his horn-rimmed glasses on his T-shirt. "Welcome to my humble home."

"Hi, Dad." Riley climbed the two wooden steps and gave him a hug. Chloe came up and kissed his cheek.

"I've been doing a little work on the place, getting ready for your first visit," Jake told them. "Come on in and I'll give you the grand tour."

"Grand?" Riley asked.

"Tour?" Chloe said. "Are you sure there's room to walk around in there?"

Jake grinned. "I know it looks small. It *is* small, but that's what I wanted—something simple. Come on." He ushered the twins into the trailer.

Riley stepped inside the main room. Or roomlet, she thought. It really was tiny. Stove, refrigerator, and microwave on one end, dining table in the middle, couch and coffee table at the other end.

Without any furniture, it might not have been so crowded. But Riley guessed that Dad didn't want things *that* simple. He'd added a shelf for his CDs and speakers, a table for his computer, and his leather swivel chair. That left about four square feet of space to stand in.

"Bedroom and bathroom are through there," Jake said, pointing to a closed door. "I'll show you later. So, how do you like it?"

"It looks…real cozy, Dad," Riley told him, hoping she sounded enthusiastic.

"Definitely!" Chloe agreed. "Nice and…simple."

Jake laughed. "Hey, I know you two probably think it's cramped, but I'm really happy here."

Riley took half a step and gave him another hug. "Then we love it, Dad."

Chloe hugged him again, too. "You said you'd done some work on it. Show us, okay?"

Jake stood by the couch and waved his arm toward the kitchen area. "Mini-blinds," he said, pointing to the window over the tiny sink. He gestured to the visible part of the floor, which was covered in white vinyl. "There used to be a shaggy green rug, but I took it up. And look." He raised the hinged coffee-table lid. Inside were a Monopoly game and a deck of cards.

"Cool, a game room," Riley joked.

Jake smiled. "And…I got you two a present."

"Dad, Chloe and I come over here because we love you," Riley told him. "Just because you and Mom separated doesn't mean you have to feel guilty and buy us presents."

"Definitely not," Chloe agreed. She paused. "Although, if you went to all that trouble, it wouldn't make any sense to let a perfectly good present go to waste, right?"

"Right." Jake laughed, took two steps, and opened the door to the bedroom.

A white puppy with a sprinkling of black hair and soft brown eyes bounded out. It yipped happily at Jake, then trotted over to Riley and Chloe, waving its tail in a circle.

"Oh, he's so cute!" Chloe cried as the puppy licked her shoe. "Is he really ours?"

"She. And, yes, she's yours," Jake said. "The people

three trailers over were selling them and I couldn't resist. She's almost four months old."

Riley sat down and pulled the puppy into her lap. "I can't believe it!" she cried as the puppy squirmed and licked her face. "I've always wanted a dog! She's adorable!"

"Well, I wanted to give you something special," Jake said. "You deserve it."

Chloe sat down next to Riley. "You're so sweet!" she said to the wriggling puppy. It crawled into her lap and licked her chin. "So, sooo sweet! Does she have a name yet, Dad?"

"I hope not," Riley said. "It'll be so much fun to name her!"

"No name yet," Jake said. "That's up to you."

"Let's take her home, Riley," Chloe said. "We can stop on the way and buy a really cute collar."

"And some toys, too," Riley added. She picked up the puppy and cuddled it under her chin. "And a bed and a leash and food."

"You might want to ask the pet store people about housebreaking dogs, too," Jake told them. "The puppy's not quite there yet."

"We'll teach her," Chloe said. "This is going to be so much fun! I can't wait to show her to Manuelo. He's going to totally love her!"

"Yeah, but Chloe?" Riley felt a sudden twinge of panic. "What do you think Mom will say?"

• • •

"Absolutely not." Macy Carlson stood in the kitchen doorway and stared at the puppy as it sniffed around the floor, checking for crumbs. "A dog? No way."

"But, Mom, we never had a pet. Not even a hamster!" Riley protested.

"And look at her!" Chloe said. "She's so adorable, how can you resist her?"

"Very easily," their mother replied. "For one thing, I'll bet she's not even house-trained."

"She is, too!" Chloe declared.

Riley gulped. Hadn't Dad said the puppy wasn't "quite there yet"? They'd have to train her fast.

"Well, that's a relief," their mother said. "But think of the hair! She'll shed all over the place."

"But her hair's short," Riley argued. "It's not like she's a collie or anything."

"Doesn't matter," her mother said. "All dogs shed. We'll be picking hair out of everything, including my designs. What on earth was your father thinking?"

Chloe sat cross-legged on the floor and pulled the puppy into her lap. "He just wanted to make us feel better," she murmured, rubbing her cheek against the dog's silky head.

[Riley: Way to go, Chloe! My sister should really think about an acting career. That sorrowful tone in her voice means she's getting ready to play

the "Dad versus Mom" card—you know, making
Mom think we might love Dad more if she doesn't
let us have something. It's not true, of course.
But it's worth a shot, especially if it means we
can keep the puppy.]

Mrs. Carlson narrowed her eyes. "What do you mean, 'feel better'?"

Chloe sighed. "Oh, you know. About the separation and everything."

Riley decided to give Chloe some backup. "We told Dad we loved him no matter what, but he wanted to do something special for us." She sat down next to her sister and let the puppy lick her fingers. "I guess he got a little carried away."

Chloe gave Riley a nudge. Riley immediately shut up. If you pushed these things too far, they could backfire.

Riley sneaked a quick glance at her mother.

Macy Carlson was frowning, but Riley could tell it wasn't a serious, put-her-foot-down frown. It was more of a what-should-she-do kind of frown.

There's definitely hope, Riley thought. She kept her head down and her mouth shut.

A minute went by.

"Well…" Macy Carlson heaved a big sigh. "If your father wanted to do this for you, I suppose I'd better go along with it."

Yes! Riley thought. As she and Chloe began to

thank her, their mother held up her hand to stop them.

"But," she said, "there are conditions attached. One, you can keep her on a trial basis only. Two, you are completely responsible for her. That means feeding, brushing, exercising—everything."

"Don't worry," Chloe assured her. "You won't have to lift a finger."

"And don't ask Manuelo to do any of it for you," their mother said. "She's your dog. Your responsibility."

"We know. This is so cool, Mom," Riley said. "Thanks."

"You're welcome." Mrs. Carlson checked her watch. "I've got to get back to work now. See you two at dinner."

After their mother left, Chloe turned to Riley. "The first thing we have to do is give her a name."

Riley shook her head. "The first thing we have to do is housebreak her."

"Good point." Chloe scratched the puppy behind its ears. "But what's the big deal? I mean, how hard can it be to train a dog?"

chapter five

"When are you going to ask your mom about an outfit?" Sierra asked Riley after school on Monday.

"Soon, I promise," Riley said. She rolled a tennis ball toward Pepper, but the puppy just looked at it.

The two of them were in Riley's driveway with Pepper. Sierra had stopped by on her way to Saul's house to rehearse. Just in case one of her parents drove by, she'd pulled her hair back into a neat ponytail, removed any trace of makeup, and wore her baggy jeans.

Riley felt awful for not asking already, but Mom had torn her fabric for the MTV dress and had to start all over. Then Mom caught Pepper chewing up her last pair of clean panty hose—in the middle of her bed. Riley could tell Mom was not in a very lending mood last week.

"How soon?" Sierra asked. "Like today?"

"I'm not sure." Riley's mother was inside, working

on her MTV creation, and Riley hadn't checked her mood yet. "I was going to ask over the weekend, but then we got Pepper and—"

"But, Riley, the concert's this coming Saturday!" Sierra cried. "That's only five days away."

"I know. Trust me, I'll ask," Riley promised. "I just have to find the right time."

"Okay," Sierra agreed reluctantly. "But don't wait too long, please?"

"Don't worry, I won't," Riley told her. She just hoped Mom was in a better frame of mind this week.

As Sierra left, Chloe came outside. "Has Pepper done anything yet?" she asked, sitting on the driveway next to the puppy.

"I'm not sure," Riley told her. "She ran around the corner of the house before and I didn't see her for a minute. Maybe she went to the bathroom then."

"Let's hope so," Chloe agreed.

Riley nodded. When it came to housebreaking, Dad was right—Pepper still wasn't "quite there" yet. Sometimes she went outside. But she'd also had a few accidents inside. Fortunately, they were all on the kitchen floor, and Riley and Chloe had cleaned them up before Mom found out.

"Hey, Chloe, what's Mom doing right now?" Riley asked, thinking of Sierra.

"Working on the MTV dress, what else?" Chloe said. "Why?"

Riley explained her promise to ask their mother about an outfit for Sierra.

"This is definitely not a good time," Chloe advised, rubbing Pepper between the ears. "Tedi called a few minutes ago. She has a cold."

Tedi was the model who'd be wearing the dress. "How sick is she?" Riley asked.

"I don't know, but she's not coming for a fitting today, and Mom's really stressing about it."

Better ask about Sierra's outfit tomorrow, Riley decided. She bent down to the puppy's water dish and wiggled her fingers in it. "Hey, Pep, aren't you getting thirsty?" she asked.

Pepper wagged her tail and nudged the tennis ball with her nose.

"She's telling you she wants to play," Chloe said. "She's so smart!"

"Yeah, but first things first, right, Pepper?" Riley said. "First drink—lots and lots of water. Then go to the bathroom—out here. Then play!"

Pepper nudged the tennis ball again.

Riley gave in with a laugh. "Okay, okay. We'll do it your way." She grabbed the tennis ball and rolled it up the driveway toward the garage. Pepper scrambled after it, yipping excitedly.

Tomorrow, Riley thought, crossing her fingers. Sierra's outfit and Pepper's housebreaking. By this time tomorrow, maybe both problems would be solved.

• • •

After school the next day, Chloe sat in the kitchen, eating a bran muffin. Riley had gone to California Dream to watch Sierra's band rehearse, and Pepper the puppy was sprawled on the floor, chewing a rawhide bone.

Manuelo stood by the refrigerator, an indignant expression on his face. "Look at me!" he said. "Tell me I don't look ridiculous!"

Chloe took a bite of muffin and gave him a critical once-over. Her mother had draped the shimmering silver material over him and pinned it in place. It was tight across the stomach and had a plunging neckline that revealed Manuelo's hairy chest.

"You don't look ridiculous exactly," Chloe said. "Just kind of—"

"Ridiculous," Manuelo repeated. "Your mother knows I am built nothing like Tedi." Because of her cold, Tedi hadn't come for a fitting today, either. "But she insisted I stand in again. She has to see how the material hangs on the human body, she says."

"You deserve an award, Manuelo," Chloe told him. "Really. Mom's so nervous, she's about ready to break into hives." She picked a raisin out of her muffin and set it aside.

"Raisins aren't cute food?" Manuelo asked, taking a sip of bottled water.

"No, they stick to your teeth." Chloe sighed. "Of course, Travis already saw my teeth blacked out with

41

chocolate frosting, so I don't know why I'm being so careful."

"There are other boys besides this Travis," Manuelo reminded her.

"But he's the one I'm interested in," Chloe said. She picked out another raisin. "He is so cool, Manuelo—like he doesn't care what anybody thinks about him. I just wish I had classes with him or something. I saw him only once yesterday and he wasn't at lunch today. Quinn's going to try to find out his class schedule for me. Then I can run into him accidentally on purpose."

"I'll keep my fingers crossed that Quinn is successful," Manuelo said.

"Manuelo, I need you, please!" Macy Carlson called from the living room.

"Modeling is not as glamorous as people think," Manuelo said, trying to flatten the hair on his chest. He put the water back in the refrigerator and turned to leave. "Ah!" He gasped. "Chloe, is that what I think it is?" He pointed to the floor.

Chloe stared at the big yellow puddle and groaned. "Pepper, I took you out half an hour ago!" she said to the dog.

Pepper cocked her head and grinned a goofy dog grin.

Chloe jumped up and grabbed a bunch of paper towels. "Please don't tell Mom about this," she begged Manuelo.

"My lips are sealed. But your mother is going to find out one of these days," Manuelo warned. "You can't keep dog pee a secret for long." He hiked up his skirt, side-stepped the puddle, and swept out the kitchen door.

Chloe mopped up the puddle, then cleaned the spot with Lysol. Pepper watched.

"You've got to work with me on this, Pepper," Chloe told the puppy. She took the leash from the hook by the door. "It's really very simple. Come on, let's go for a walk and I'll try to explain it again."

As she led the puppy out the door, Chloe sighed a little. Actually, nothing was as simple as she thought it would be. So far, she was striking out with Pepper *and* with Travis.

A few blocks away, Riley sat on the patio at California Dream, listening as The Wave rehearsed for its big Saturday night performance.

California Dream was located right on the beach. And it was one of the most popular places in town. It booked name bands, but it also showcased amateur groups. Even ones from high school like The Wave got a chance to perform.

The café had booths inside, and tables outside on the patio and deck. Part of the deck jutted out over the sand, and that's where the band would perform. People who couldn't get tables sat on the beach.

Sitting with Saul's friends Joelle and Carrie, Riley

sipped a lemonade and watched the band. Blond-haired Saul was on drums. Marta, wearing a red bandanna around her head, played the keyboard. Alex was on lead guitar and sometimes sang. Sierra was on bass.

Except for her clothes, Sarah was in full Sierra mode, strutting around the deck and singing in a rich, throaty voice.

"She has such a great voice," Joelle said. "It's really too bad her parents hear it only when she sings in the chorus."

"Yeah, I wish they'd loosen up a little," Carrie agreed. "Sierra's going to be famous someday, I bet. What are they going to do, not come to see her?"

With a crash of drums and the high whine of an electric guitar, the song came to an end. Riley and her friends clapped loudly.

"Hey, how'd we sound?" Saul called out.

"Awesome. Totally," Joelle replied. She and Carrie climbed onto the deck and went to talk to the band.

Sierra set her guitar down and came over to Riley. "I don't have much time, so listen—did you ask your mom?"

"Not yet," Riley admitted.

"Riley, you promised!" Sierra cried.

"I know, and I'll still ask!" Riley insisted. Of course, she didn't know when exactly.

"Please, Riley," Sierra said. "I have to wear something cool—I just have to! Look, your mom can't be stressed every single minute of the day, right?" she asked.

"You don't know my mom," Riley told her.

"Maybe not, but I know you can find a good time to ask," Sierra said. "Catch her when she's sleepy or something. Or—I know! Give her a present, like flowers. Then when you ask, she'll say yes. Please, Riley! This is so important!"

Riley couldn't argue. It *was* important and she *had* promised. Maybe a present was a good idea. "Don't worry, Sierra," she said. "I'll ask her. You'll definitely have something cool to wear."

"Thanks, Riley." Sierra glanced over her shoulder. "I've got to get back now. Don't forget to ask—soon!"

As the band continued to practice, the smell of baking sourdough bread began to drift out to the patio. Riley's stomach growled. She decided to go home and get something to eat. Then she'd think about what kind of present she could get to butter up Mom.

Halfway home, she met Chloe and Pepper strolling along the sidewalk. Chloe turned around and began walking back with Riley. "How's the rehearsal going?" she asked.

"Great," Riley said.

Chloe peered at her. "So how come you look so worried?"

"I still haven't asked Mom about lending an outfit to Sierra," Riley explained, "and Sierra's freaking out. What kind of mood was Mom in when you left?"

"I'm not sure. Tedi's still really sick," Chloe reported. Riley groaned.

"But Manuelo is standing in for her again," Chloe said. "He's not thrilled about it, but at least Mom's getting some work done. That always makes her happy."

"So maybe I should get her a bunch of flowers or some candy and then ask," Riley said. "I'll check the situation when we get home. What about Pepper?" she asked. "Has she figured out where she's supposed to go to the bathroom yet?"

"Don't ask. Maybe you'll have better luck with her when you walk her tonight."

The puppy suddenly stopped. It stared off to its right and gave a little yip.

"What is it, Pepper?" Chloe asked. "What do you see?"

"Uh-oh." Riley pointed down the sidewalk.

Larry had just rounded the corner. When he spotted Riley and Chloe, he waved. "Hi, Chloe! Hi, Riley!" he shouted. "Hey, Riley, will you go out with me?"

"No, Larry," Riley called back automatically.

"I knew you'd say that." With a grin, Larry hurried toward them. "Hey, is that your dog?"

Riley nodded and picked the puppy up. "Dad gave her to us. Her name's Pepper."

"Hi, Pepper," Larry said. "Hey, Pepper, maybe you can get Riley to go out with me."

Riley rolled her eyes.

As Larry reached out to pet Pepper, the puppy yipped. "Whoa!" Larry drew his hand back. "Is she a biter?"

"Um…" Riley knew Pepper was just being friendly, but this was a good excuse to get away from Larry. She just wasn't in the mood for the asking-out game at the moment. "I don't think so," she said. "But I'm not a hundred percent sure."

"Oh. Well, she's cute, but I guess I won't take any chances," Larry said.

"Good idea," Riley told him. "Listen, we have to go. See you, Larry."

Riley tucked Pepper under her arm and waved good-bye. Then she and Chloe hurried home.

"Hi, Mom," she said, setting the puppy down in the living room.

Their mother was actually sitting on the couch, doing nothing. Was that a good sign or a bad sign? Riley wondered.

"Hi, you two," Mrs. Carlson said with a smile.

The smile is a good sign, Riley thought. "How's the dress going?" she asked.

Mrs. Carlson laughed. "It's actually going well, even though Manuelo isn't Tedi. I'm starting to feel very good about it."

Great, Riley thought. Forget the flowers—Mom's smiling and the dress is going well. Now's the right time to ask. "Mom?" she said. "Could I ask you something?"

"OH, NO! RILEY! CHLOE!" her mother suddenly shrieked.

"What?" Riley asked, confused.

"Look!" Mrs. Carlson cried. "Just look at the rug!"

Riley looked. "Oh, no" was right. Pepper had done it again.

Okay, so this wasn't a good time to ask after all.

chapter six

"I'm really sorry, Mom," Riley said. What a disaster, she thought. "I don't know why Pepper did that. I mean, we just had her outside, right, Chloe?"

Chloe nodded. "I walked her down the beach and she did everything she was supposed to."

"Obviously, not everything," their mother said.

"Don't worry, we'll clean it up," Riley assured her.

"Right. You'll never know she did anything," Chloe said. "Really. I saw some stuff at the pet store and it's guaranteed to take out the stain *and* the smell."

"Great!" Riley said. "Come on, Chloe. Let's go buy some now."

"Good idea," their mother said. "Clean up the mess, then take the dog straight back to your father."

"What?" Riley cried. She couldn't believe it. "Mom, you can't mean that."

"That is *so* not fair!" Chloe protested. "It's not

Pepper's fault that she had one tiny, little accident."

"Of course it's not," their mother agreed. "It's not really yours, either. I know you've been trying, but it isn't working. Pepper's been having accidents all over the house. She's been eating my clothes, knocking over the garbage…and I've got too much on my mind. I just can't worry about the dog, too."

"But the MTV dress will be finished in a few days," Riley reminded her. "And you said it was going well."

"Yes, but, honey, that's now," their mother said. "Who knows what'll happen tomorrow? The dog has to go."

Riley groaned. Mom sounded like her mind was made up. "I can't believe this! You actually want us to kick Pepper out just because she had a few little accidents? She's our pet! We love her!"

Chloe picked up the puppy. "Don't worry, Pepper, we won't kick you out," she murmured, kissing the puppy's head. "If Mom doesn't want you, I guess we'll just have to go live with Dad."

[Riley: Chloe sounds like she means it, doesn't she? Fortunately, I know she doesn't really want to move in with Dad. It's just a bluff. But didn't I tell you she was a good actress?]

"Fine," Mrs. Carlson said.

[Riley: Whoa. I didn't expect Mom to say that. But she's bluffing, too. I can always tell. Hey, maybe that's where Chloe gets her talent.]

"Huh?" Chloe asked. "What did you say?"

"Fine," her mother repeated. "I know you're very attached to Pepper, and I know your father misses having you around all the time. I think it's a great idea to move in with him. You and the puppy can come back after the MTV awards. Problem solved."

Smiling cheerfully, Mrs. Carlson left the living room.

"I can't believe she said that," Riley declared. "I was positive she was bluffing."

"Me, too," Chloe admitted. "I was, that's for sure. So what do we do now?"

Riley hesitated. "Well, we can't cave," she decided. "I mean, we've taken a stand—if Pepper goes, we go. So let's pack."

"Ummph! Riley, get off me!" Chloe muttered sleepily on Thursday morning. "You're lying on top of my arm."

"Huh? Oh, sorry." Riley rolled over on the trailer's lumpy pull-out couch.

Chloe's arm began to tingle. She yawned, rolled over, and fell to the floor. "Ow!"

"Are you okay?" Riley asked, peering over the edge of the mattress.

"I think so." Chloe sat up, rubbing her arm. "How long have we been staying in the trailer?"

"We got here Tuesday night. This is Thursday morning," Riley said with yawn. "I guess Mom was serious after all. She hasn't called to tell us to come back home."

Chloe pushed her hair out of her eyes and glanced around the trailer's tiny main room. It hadn't grown any bigger. "Oh, well, we won't be here much longer," she said. "And Dad said he'd sleep in here tonight so we can have the futon in the bedroom. I'm sure that will be more comfortable."

"Right," Riley said. "Want to flip to see who showers first?"

The bedroom door opened and Jake walked into the living room. He wore his usual shorts and T-shirt and his hair was still wet from the shower. "Morning, girls," he said cheerfully. "How'd you sleep?"

"Great!" Chloe told him. Actually, the couch had the absolute worst mattress she'd ever slept on, but she didn't want to hurt her dad's feelings. "Riley and I were just going to flip a coin for the shower."

"Ah, well, you might want to take a quick one this morning," Jake said. "I'm afraid the hot water ran out again. I'll start timing my showers tomorrow. Promise."

"Don't worry about it, Dad," Chloe told him cheerfully. "No big deal. I'll just wash my face. I mean, who needs to shower every single morning?"

[Chloe: I know. YOU do. But, hey, I'm trying to be optimistic here, okay?]

"Right. Just think of all the water we've been wasting," Riley agreed. "You can have the bathroom first, Chloe. I'll feed Pepper." Pepper was outside. As long as it didn't rain, they'd tied her to the deck steps on a long lead, where she could move around and have all the accidents she wanted.

> [Chloe: Riley, on the other hand, is naturally optimistic when it comes to this kind of stuff. She says it reminds her of camping. I hate camping.]

"And I'll take my morning walk, do a little meditating on the beach," Jake said. "Hey, it's really good to have you guys here!" he added. "It's a little crowded, but it's fun. You know what it reminds me of?"

Chloe drew a blank. Living out of duffel bags and being so cramped didn't remind her of anything fun.

"It reminds me of when we used to go camping!" Jake said.

"Oh, riiiight," Chloe agreed with a big (fake) smile.

"See you later!" Dad went out the door.

Chloe grabbed her toothbrush, hairbrush, and makeup from the coffee table and went into the bedroom. With her back against the wall, she skirted the futon and entered the small bathroom.

At the tiny sink, she brushed her teeth and washed her face in cold water. Then she took a deep breath and gazed into the mirror.

Ugh. This was the worst case of bedhead hair she'd ever seen. The part she could actually *see*, anyway. The mirror was so small, she had to look at herself in sections.

Chloe moved a few inches to the left. Great. This

side stuck out and the other side was mashed. And there was no hot water, no time to wash and blow-dry her hair.

She brushed the sticking-out side, but it sprang right up again. She tried to fluff the mashed side, but it flopped back down. She gave up and brushed it all over, put on some lip gloss, and stumbled back into the main room.

"Okay, I just fed Pepper—whoa!" Riley said. "What did you do to your hair?"

"Don't ask," Chloe said, putting on a wrinkled skirt and a short-sleeved red sweater. "Riley, look at me. I can't let Travis see me like this. Quinn finally got his schedule for me, and I was going to wait outside his sixth-period class today."

"Why don't you just dunk your head under the water and then comb it out straight?" Riley suggested.

"That never works," Chloe said. She glanced at the clock above the mini-stove. "And there's not enough time to blow it dry. Riley, we can't stay here anymore! Can't we just leave Pepper here until the MTV awards?"

"No," Riley argued. "We can't give in to Mom."

"Please, Riley?" Chloe pleaded. "I mean, you don't really like staying here, do you?"

"No," Riley admitted. "But what about Pepper?"

"Dad won't mind taking care of her for a few more days," Chloe said. "He'll probably be glad if we go. I mean, he's being really nice about it, but I bet he's feeling crowded, too."

"I know, but I really hate to go crawling home," Riley said reluctantly.

"Yeah, but we'll be crawling home to a hot shower and a comfortable bed," Chloe reminded her. "Look, I'll go talk to Dad while you're in the bathroom."

Not bothering to put on her shoes, Chloe opened the trailer door and stepped onto the deck.

Pepper barked a greeting from the bottom of the steps. Chloe trotted down and patted the puppy's head as she scanned the beach for her father.

There he was, walking on the wet sand. Chloe started to head that way, when a rumbling noise made her jump. She glanced over her shoulder.

A red dirt bike was moving along the path that wound among the trailers. The rider wore a helmet, but that didn't keep Chloe from recognizing him.

It was Travis.

When he passed behind her dad's trailer, Chloe dashed to the other end and peered out.

Travis rumbled along the path, then turned in at the next trailer. He killed the engine and climbed off, hanging his helmet on the handlebars.

Chloe waited. Travis hurried up the short path and entered the trailer. He came back out a few seconds later, carrying a couple of spiral notebooks. He stuffed them in the bike's saddlebag, gunned the motor to life, and rode away.

Chloe couldn't believe it! Travis Morgan actually lived

in the next trailer! She hadn't seen him yesterday. He must have left early and come home late or something.

Chloe grinned. Moving in with Dad was the best thing they'd ever done! "Riley!" she shouted. "Hurry and come out here! Quick!"

Still wearing the big blue T-shirt she'd slept in, Riley banged open the door and hurried onto the deck. "What's wrong?"

"Nothing! Everything's right!" Chloe cried. "And guess what? We're not leaving."

"Huh? Why not?"

Chloe pointed to the next trailer. "Because Travis Morgan is our next-door neighbor, that's why!"

"You're kidding, right?" Riley said.

Chloe shook her head no. "I just saw him. He rode up on his bike and went in. When he came out, he had some notebooks with him. He must have forgotten them. That's his home, Riley. Right next door to Dad!"

"So you want us to stay in this tiny little box, getting mashed hair and claustrophobia, just because of Travis," Riley said.

"But just a minute ago you said you didn't want to go crawling home," Chloe reminded her.

"I know. But I was just getting used to the idea of sleeping in my own bed again," Riley said.

"Well, you can leave if you want to," Chloe told her. "I guess it's a question of what's worse—staying in Dad's trailer or letting Mom win."

[Riley: She's good, isn't she? Chloe knows I don't want to stay. But she also knows I don't want to give in to Mom. What's more important—standing under a hot shower or standing on my principles?]

"Oh, please, Riley!" Chloe said. "If you go home, I won't have anybody to talk to. Besides, haven't you noticed something?"

"What?" Riley asked.

"Larry," Chloe replied. "He hasn't shown up once. He hasn't figured out where you are."

[Riley: Yup. She is good. I didn't even realize that it's been one whole day without Larry asking me out. It's kinda nice.]

"Okay," Riley agreed. "We stay."

chapter
seven

After school on Thursday, Chloe hurried back to the trailer and changed into white shorts and a neon-pink top. She thought about washing her hair but was afraid to waste the time. She'd tied it back in the school bathroom that morning, and it still looked okay.

"I'm going to sit outside with the dog, Dad," she told her father.

"Fine, honey," Jake called from his room.

Barefoot, Chloe stepped out onto the deck and checked the trailer next door. The dirt bike wasn't there.

Come on, Travis, Chloe thought. Where *are* you?

Chloe hadn't seen him since that morning. He wasn't in the cafeteria or on the quad at lunch. Quinn had gotten his schedule, but when Chloe rushed to his sixth-period classroom, only the English teacher was there. She'd sent everyone to the library to do research. Chloe's next class was way on the other side of the building, and there was no time to make it to the library.

Come on, Travis, Chloe thought again. Please don't be staying over at a friend's or something.

She untied Pepper from the deck railing and walked the puppy around a little bit, keeping an eye out for Travis. Pepper wandered every which way, tangling the leash around Chloe's ankles at least five times.

Chloe tugged on the leash and said "Heel" and "No." She tried praising and scolding and begging, but the dog seemed totally oblivious. Finally Chloe decided to take a break.

As she retied Pepper, she heard the sputtering putt-putt of an engine. She climbed the steps and stared down the path.

Yes! It was Travis. Chloe hurried to the other end of the deck and watched as he rode up to the trailer next door. The bike's sputtering turned into a cough, and finally the engine died.

Travis climbed off and gazed at the bike, shaking his head. He went into his trailer and was back out in a minute, carrying a toolbox.

Perfect, Chloe thought. While Travis worked on his bike, she'd place herself in full view. He'd have to look up once in a while. When he saw her, she'd wave. He'd be so surprised to see her next door, he'd have to say something.

And that would be the beginning of their relationship.

Chloe grabbed a towel from one of the rickety aluminum deck chairs and draped it over the wooden railing so she wouldn't get any splinters. Although a splinter might work as a last resort. She could ask Travis to pull it out.

Travis was kneeling by his bike, doing something to it with a wrench. Chloe climbed onto the railing. It was a little narrow, but she finally managed to sit without wobbling. She drew her knees up and wrapped her arms around them.

And waited.

Metal banged on metal. Travis sighed loudly.

Chloe deliberately didn't look at him. She tilted her head back and gazed at the sky.

And waited some more.

More metal noises. Another sigh. Then a lot of loud clanking.

Chloe sneaked a look.

Travis had his head down and was searching through the toolbox.

Chloe carefully rearranged her position, stretching out one leg and leaning back on her elbows. Maybe the movement of her bright pink top would catch his eye.

She sneaked another look.

Travis was still concentrating on the stupid bike.

Chloe decided to fake a cough. As she did, the engine started up, drowning her out. Fortunately, it sputtered twice, then gave up again.

In the silence, Chloe coughed again. Travis crouched over the toolbox and didn't even glance her way.

Chloe groaned to herself. This was totally frustrating. Still, she couldn't give up yet. She shifted into another pose. A real model-type pose, something Travis couldn't miss.

Moving as gracefully as possible, Chloe stretched her other leg out, turned on her side, and rolled like a log off the railing. "Umph!"

As she plopped facedown into the soft sand, Chloe tried to tell herself this wasn't so bad. Travis must have seen her fall. He'd hurry over and ask if she was okay.

And that would be the beginning of their relationship.

The bike's engine growled and hacked.

Chloe scrambled to her feet and looked across the way. Travis hadn't even turned his head.

Okay, this isn't working, Chloe thought. She needed another plan. Spitting sand, she walked over to the puppy and gave her a pat.

Pepper licked Chloe's hand, then nudged a tennis ball lying in the sand near the bottom step.

That's it! Chloe thought. She'd play with Pepper for a minute, then try to train her to the leash. Travis would notice and come over to talk.

And *that* would be the beginning of their relationship. After all, who could resist a puppy?

Chloe untied Pepper, then rolled the tennis ball

away from her. "Okay, Pepper, go and get it!" she cried.

Pepper dashed after the ball, snarling and yipping. It was too big for her to take in her mouth, so she nudged it back with her nose.

"Good girl!" Chloe said. She glanced at Travis. He hadn't looked up from the bike yet. "Want to do it again, Pepper?" Chloe asked loudly.

Pepper yipped. Chloe rolled the ball. The puppy chased after it. Chloe laughed and chased after the puppy.

Travis ignored the entire scene.

"Now it's time for some work, Pepper!" Chloe told the dog. Maybe if Travis saw that she was having trouble training the puppy, he'd come over and help.

Chloe snapped the leash onto Pepper's collar. "Okay, Pepper, heel!" she said. She started to walk.

The puppy nudged the tennis ball.

"No," Chloe said. "Playtime is over. Come on, Pepper, heel!"

Pepper sat down.

"Come on!" Chloe coaxed, tugging gently on the leash. "Come on, Pepper!"

Pepper yawned and stretched out on her stomach.

Chloe glanced over at Travis. He was still working on his bike. Pepper was dozing. Great. Now she couldn't even get a dog's attention.

Chloe took off the leash and attached the long lead to Pepper's collar again, then went into the trailer.

Dad was sitting at his computer. He looked up. "You're all sandy. What happened?"

"Don't ask." Chloe sighed and flopped on the couch. "Dad, do you know the boy who lives in the next trailer?"

"The kid with the dirt bike?" he asked. "Not really."

Chloe nodded. "His name is Travis and he goes to my school. I keep trying to get him to notice me, but it's not happening. And Pepper totally ignores me, too. I feel like a total failure."

"Well, I'm not sure what to tell you about this Travis," Jake said. "But when I bought the puppy I ordered a book over the Internet. Sort of a beginner's guide to dog training. It came today and I forgot to give it to you. Here, it's in my library."

Dad's library was a tiny shelf above his computer with three books on it. One was on Zen meditation and one was on finding your true inner self. Dad took the third one down and handed it to Chloe.

"Thanks, Dad," Chloe said, flipping through the pages. "I'll go try it out now. I just wish there was a book on training a boy."

Leaving her father at his computer, Chloe went back outside and began to study the book. "'Eye contact,'" she read. "'Establish dominance by getting your dog to blink first.'"

Chloe read a few more pages, then decided to try out a couple of commands. She untied Pepper and walked a few steps away. The puppy started to follow.

Chloe turned to face the dog. "Stay," she commanded. She held her palm out, put a stern expression on her face, and stared the dog in the eye. "Stay."

Pepper stopped walking.

"Whoa, I don't believe it," Chloe said. "Good dog, Pepper!"

Next, Chloe went over to Pepper and pushed down on her rear end. "Sit," she said. The dog sat, then stood up again. "Sit," Chloe repeated, still maintaining eye contact.

Pepper plopped down on the deck.

"Good dog!" Chloe grinned and petted her. "Okay, Pepper, speak!" she commanded.

The puppy kept quiet, but a nearby voice said, "Hi."

Chloe spun around. Travis Morgan was sitting by his dirt bike, gazing at her.

Chloe stared back, totally surprised. Then she glanced at the dog-training book in her hand. No way, she thought. No *way* this book could work on a boy…could it? She had to try again.

"Speak," she told Pepper.

"Hi," Travis repeated, still sitting by his dirtbike.

[Chloe: I know this seems crazy and impossible. But how else do you explain it?]

Chloe looked back at Travis. "Hi," she said with a smile.

chapter
eight

When Riley got back to the trailer, she found Chloe waiting for her on the deck, practically jumping up and down with excitement. "Wait till you hear!" Chloe announced. "You are not going to believe it!"

"You changed your mind and we're moving back to the house?" Riley guessed hopefully.

"Even better!"

"We're moving back anyway because you found out Travis was only visiting that trailer?" Riley asked.

"No. Listen!" Chloe cried. "He talked to me. Travis and I actually had a conversation!"

"You did!" Riley squealed. "What did he say?"

"He said, 'Hi,'" Chloe replied.

"Then what?" Riley asked eagerly.

"Well," Chloe said. "He said 'Hi' again."

Riley tilted her head. "That's it? 'Hi'?"

Chloe nodded. "And I owe it all to this book." She

showed Riley the dog-training book. "It worked on Pepper *and* on Travis!"

While Chloe described the whole scene, Riley checked out a few of the training tips. They made sense—for a dog, anyway. "You're joking about Travis, right?" she asked.

"I am *serious*," Chloe insisted. "Weren't you listening? Travis said 'hi.' And when I looked at him, he was *sitting down*. And this was after I'd just done the sit command with Pepper."

Riley rolled her eyes. "So you put two and two together..."

"Exactly," Chloe agreed.

"Give me a break," Riley told her. She sat in one of the deck chairs. "It had to be a coincidence, Chloe. I mean, how can you compare boys to dogs?"

"Think about it," Chloe said. "They both follow you around. They both growl when you take away their food. And they both scratch themselves in front of company."

Riley laughed but shook her head. The whole thing was ridiculous. "I'm still not buying it, Chloe. Boys are human beings."

"What about Larry?" Chloe asked.

"Larry's an exception," Riley said as she got up. "Anyway, good luck with training Travis. I have to go to the house."

"What for?"

Riley glanced around. "Promise you won't say a word to anybody?"

"Sure, if you promise to bring back my new yellow top," Chloe agreed. "I want to wear it tomorrow. It's in the second drawer of my dresser."

"Deal." Riley glanced around again. "Sierra's meeting me at the house," she confided in a whisper.

"Why are you whispering?" Chloe asked. Then her eyes widened. "Oh, wait. You're not going to take one of Mom's designs without asking, are you?"

"I don't know what else to do," Riley said. "I promised Sierra I'd ask, only now I'm too chicken. And I've put it off until the last minute. If Mom says no now, Sierra will have nothing to wear.

"Don't do it, Riley," Chloe warned. "If Mom finds out, you'll be grounded for life."

Riley groaned. "Don't remind me."

Chloe thought a second. "I know—why don't you let Sierra take a scarf or a belt or something instead of a whole outfit? Mom would never miss something like that."

[**Riley**: Why didn't I think of that? Maybe older— even eight minutes older—really does mean wiser!]

"Chloe, you're a genius!" Riley cried.

When Riley got to the house, she found Sierra waiting outside. "I'm so excited!" Sierra declared. "Thank you so much for helping me, Riley. I really owe you big for this."

"Don't thank me yet," Riley told her. She quickly explained her decision not to take an entire outfit. "I know I promised, but I never found the right time to ask Mom. Now, after Pepper and everything, I just can't risk taking one of her designs. I would be in major, major trouble."

"But, Riley, what am I going to wear?" Sierra wailed.

Riley quickly explained Chloe's idea of "borrowing" something like a belt or a scarf.

"A scarf? A belt?" Sierra cried. "What else am I supposed to wear?"

Riley hated disappointing her friend. There had to be some way to get her an outfit.

"All I have in my locker are jeans," Sierra went on. "I guess I could wear them, but..."

"Wait!" Riley cried. "I just remembered something—your black leather pants are still in my closet!"

Sierra had bought the pants for a party, and they were so tight, they looked painted on. Riley kept them in her closet, so Sierra's parents wouldn't discover them.

"You're right!" Sierra said. "I can definitely wear those. And on top..." She frowned. "None of my tops are right!"

Riley suddenly remembered something else. "Chloe has the perfect top!" she said. "It's cropped and sleeveless and yellow, with little silver sequins around the neck. It'll go great with the pants. I'll check with Chloe, but I'm sure she won't mind." At least I *hope* she won't mind, Riley thought.

"Great!" Sierra said.

Relieved that she hadn't let her friend down, Riley opened the front door and stuck her head in. "Hello!" she called. "Anybody home?"

No answer. Good. Her mother was probably out somewhere, and this was one of Manuelo's days off. "Come on," she said to Sierra. "Let's see what we can find."

Riley led Sierra through the living room and into the den, which was where Mrs. Carlson worked. A long wooden table was covered with the silvery material of her latest design. A sewing machine stood against one wall, a clothing rack against another. Dresses, blouses, scarves, and belts hung from the rack. Lengths of material were draped over chairs. There were pairs of shoes all over, some in boxes, some lined up against the walls.

"See what you can find," Riley told Sierra. "Just don't touch the stuff on the table. I'll go get the top."

Riley ran upstairs, took Chloe's new yellow top from the dresser and Sierra's leather pants from her closet. Then she ran back downstairs.

"Look!" Sierra said when Riley returned to the den. She held out a pair of slides. The heels were as thin as pencils and about four inches high. The wide straps were crusted with glittering rhinestones.

"Aren't these cool?" Sierra asked. "I found them in the back of your mom's closet. It's like they were made for what I'm wearing." She slipped them on. "And they fit, too!"

"That's great," Riley said. "Okay, mission accomplished. Let's go before Mom comes home."

Safely out of the house, Riley gave Sierra the pants and the sparkling top.

"Thanks, Riley," Sierra said, folding the clothes and putting them in her backpack. "I'm going to look great."

"You are," Riley agreed. "See you tomorrow!"

"Bye, Riley!" Sierra waved and headed home.

Riley started walking back to Dad's trailer.

As she turned onto the road leading to the park, she heard footsteps behind her. She turned.

It was Larry. Why was she not surprised?

"Hi, Riley!" Larry said.

"Hi, Larry." Riley waited for him to ask her out, as she usually did.

Instead, Larry said, "Where have you been?"

Oh. Right. She'd forgotten that he didn't know. "Um…"

"You're never home anymore," Larry told her. "Your mom's too busy to talk to me, and all Manuelo says is, 'She's around somewhere.' But you're not. Where are you?"

"Oh, you know…" Riley said. "I've been here and there. Busy and everything. I guess you just missed me."

"I sure did," Larry told her. "Hey, Riley, will you go out with me?"

Well, at least they were back to the game, Riley thought. "No, Larry," she said with a laugh. "Listen, I have to go, okay?" Riley began moving away.

"Hey, I'll walk with you," Larry said, starting after her.

Oh, no. Now what? Riley wondered. If Larry walked with her to Vista del Car, he'd know where she was staying. Then he'd start hanging around there all the time.

She had to stop Larry from following her. The question was, how? She didn't want to yell at him. And she couldn't just order him to stop in his tracks.

Or could she?

[Riley: I know you heard me tell Chloe it was crazy, but I'm desperate. I have to give it a try.]

Riley stopped walking and whirled around. Holding her hand out, she looked straight into Larry's eyes and said, "Stay!"

"Huh?" Larry frowned, but he began to slow down.

"Stay!" Riley repeated.

"Well...okay." Larry shrugged and came to a stop. He gazed back at her, an expectant look on his face.

Riley remembered a sentence from the dog-training book—"When your dog obeys a command, lavish him with praise."

Riley grinned. "Thanks, Larry. That's really great! Now just stay there, okay?"

Larry shrugged again. "Okay. If you say so."

Riley took a few steps backward, then turned and walked briskly away. When she glanced back, Larry was still standing in the same spot, gazing at her wistfully.

Amazed, Riley walked on. Maybe Chloe was on to something after all.

chapter
nine

"Is Chloe okay with me borrowing her top?" Sierra asked Riley as they walked down the hall at school on Friday.

"Yeah, she's fine with it," Riley assured her. "How does it look?"

"Awesome!" Sierra replied. "I tried it on with the pants and shoes last night after Mom and Dad went to bed, and the whole outfit is totally perfect. Thanks for helping me out. And thank Chloe for me, okay? See you later!"

Sierra hurried toward her next class. Riley had a free period and hadn't decided where to go. Library? Study hall? The cafeteria? She needed to do some research for an English paper. She had a math test coming up. And she was hungry.

She could do research on Dad's computer. And the math test wasn't until next week. She could already smell lunch—pizza and chicken fingers. No contest, she thought. Food wins.

As Riley turned down the hall toward the cafeteria, Larry popped out from behind his locker door. "Hi, Riley!"

"Hi, Larry." Riley gave him a little wave and kept walking.

Larry hurried to catch up. "Hey, Riley, will you go out with me?" he asked.

"No, Larry—I bet you knew I'd say that," she told him.

"Yeah, but I'm going to keep asking." Larry grinned and nudged her playfully with his shoulder. Unfortunately, he nudged a little too hard.

Riley stumbled sideways and bumped into a bunch of kids coming around the corner. "Hey, watch it," a guy said as she tripped over his foot.

"Sorry." Riley stumbled again and lost her balance. As the other kids swept past, she reached out to grab something, but there was nothing to grab. Her backpack slid off her shoulder and across the hall. Riley tried to go after it, but she was still off balance and crashed into a locker.

"Sorry about that, Riley," Larry said from the other side of the hall. "You okay?"

"Just great, Larry." Riley rubbed her shoulder and winced. "What happened to my backpack?"

"It's right here." Larry bent down to pick up the bag.

"Be careful, it's not..." Riley started to say.

But Larry had already scooped it up—by the wrong end. A notebook and pens fell onto the floor.

"...zipped," Riley finished.

"Don't worry, I'll get them!" Larry assured her. Scrambling after the rolling pens, he managed to step on the notebook, which had opened when it fell.

"Those are my history notes!" Riley cried, rushing across the hall.

"Sorry." Larry took his foot off the notebook and stepped on a pen, cracking it in half. "Sorry!"

"Larry!" Riley said, exasperated. She felt like screaming at him. Then she suddenly remembered the dog-training book. "No," she declared in a firm voice. "Stay where you are. Don't move. Stay."

Larry looked at her. He started to say something, but Riley held her hand out and shook her head. "No," she said again.

Larry closed his mouth and didn't move.

Riley took the backpack from him, then picked up her notebook and pens and shoved them inside. "That was great, Larry," she said, remembering that praise was important. "Thanks!"

Giving Larry a big smile, Riley sped down the hall and into the cafeteria. She waited inside the door for a moment, but Larry didn't appear. If he'd moved, at least he hadn't moved in her direction.

This dog-training stuff was unbelievable, she

thought. Glancing around, she spotted Chloe sitting at a table with Amanda Gray. Well, not *with*, exactly. Amanda was at one end and Chloe was at the other.

Riley bought a slice of pizza and joined her sister. She said "hi" to Amanda. Amanda smiled shyly and went back to her chicken fingers.

"You don't have lunch now," Chloe said.

"Free period. And I was starving." Riley bit the point off her pizza slice and used her fingers to pull the stringy cheese into her mouth.

"That's disgusting," Chloe told her, sticking a straw into her Sprite. "You're going to have cheese and tomato sauce all over your teeth."

Riley chewed and swallowed. "It's worth it. Anyway, forget about my teeth. You will never believe what happened."

"What?"

"You know the dog-training book?" Riley asked.

"Sure." Chloe leaned down and pulled it out of her backpack. A couple of sheets of notes came with it, so she folded them into the back of the book. "I brought it with me so I could learn some more tips. What about it?"

"I thought you were nuts, but you were right," Riley said. "I tried the stay command on Larry yesterday when I was coming back from the house—and it worked!"

"I told you it did." Chloe laughed. "Why didn't you tell me about this last night?"

"I just couldn't believe it. I thought it might be a

weird coincidence or something," Riley explained. "But just before I came in here, Larry showed up and I tried the same command—with the *same* result!"

As Riley described how she'd held out her hand and commanded Larry to stay, she noticed that Amanda was listening. Holding a chicken finger halfway to her lips, the quiet girl gazed back and forth between Chloe and Riley.

Amanda probably thinks we're crazy, Riley decided. No wonder—we're actually talking about using a dog-training book on boys. How weird is that?

"I wonder if Larry's still standing where you left him," Chloe said. She began flipping through the dog book. "I saw a release command somewhere in here. Oh, right—you clap your hands and say 'Okay.'"

"I don't think he needs to be released," Riley told her. "He can come out of it by himself. He must have done it last night, because he's at school today."

"I guess you're right." Chloe giggled. "Let's go check him out, anyway. I'm dying to see if—oh!" She gasped. "He's here!"

"Already?" Riley glanced around, expecting to see Larry looking for her. But Larry was nowhere in sight.

Instead, she spotted Travis Morgan winding his way through the crowded tables.

Riley looked at Chloe. Leaning back in her chair, her sister had pasted a bright smile on her face. Her eyes sparkled and every tooth gleamed.

"He doesn't notice me," Chloe said, barely moving her lips. "What should I do?"

"What were we just discussing?" Riley asked impatiently. She tapped the dog book. "It works, remember? Use it!"

"Right, right!" Chloe clutched the book to her chest.

"Remember—sharp, crisp commands. Don't lose eye contact," Riley reminded her. "Stare him down."

Chloe nodded. "I'll show him who his master is. Here goes!"

Chloe stood up, still holding the book. As Travis drew closer to the table, she sucked up a big mouthful of Sprite. Riley tried to stop her, but it was too late.

As Chloe stepped into Travis's path, the icy drink suddenly hit. Riley watched helplessly as her sister went into a brain freeze.

"Ahhh!" Chloe moaned in agony and pressed her thumb between her eyes.

Travis stopped in his tracks, startled at the sight.

Riley didn't think it was possible for Chloe to move, but she did. Clutching the book to her chest, she staggered forward. She stared at Travis with a fierce expression and muttered to herself, "Maintain eye contact. Maintain eye contact."

Travis backed up a step. He was looking a little scared now, and Riley couldn't blame him. Chloe looked totally crazed.

Slowly, Chloe advanced on Travis. Step by step, she

backed him across the cafeteria and out into the hall.

Riley scooted out from her table and followed. Amanda was right on her heels, carrying a half-eaten chicken finger. A crowd of kids gathered in the hall, laughing and curious.

Travis risked a glance over his shoulder. Behind him was a door. With a last panicky look at Chloe, he backed inside. The door swung shut behind him.

Riley watched in amazement as her sister, completely concentrating on her mission, stiff-armed the big door and followed Travis straight into the boys' bathroom.

Oh, no! Riley thought. Chloe was going to be totally mortified.

"Ahhh!" Chloe screamed, bursting out of the boys' bathroom two seconds after she'd gone in.

"Way to go, Chloe!" a voice shouted.

"Yeah, nice show." Someone laughed. "What'd you do to Travis?"

Oh, no! Chloe thought, glancing around. Everybody was looking at her, grinning and laughing.

Chloe's cheeks burned. This was *so* embarrassing! The best thing to do would be to die right on the spot. The next best thing was to disappear.

"What's going on here?" a man called out loudly.

Chloe jumped and dropped the dog-training book on the floor. Glancing around, she saw Vice Principal

Connor pushing his way through the laughing crowd.

Connor was short and plump, with a nasal voice that squeaked when he tried to yell. "I said, what's going on here?" he repeated.

All the kids put on innocent expressions and shook their heads. Chloe breathed a sigh of relief. At least no one was going to rat on her.

"All right, let's break it up, then," Connor said, clapping his hands. "The show's over, whatever it was. Get back to class."

The crowd broke up and began to drift away. Chloe spotted Riley and hurried over to her. "That was absolutely the most humiliating moment of my life!" She groaned.

Riley patted Chloe's shoulder sympathetically. "I know, but don't worry about it. It's over, right?"

Still blushing with embarrassment, Chloe turned around and saw Travis picking a book up from the floor.

The dog-training book.

No! Chloe thought. She couldn't let him get his hands on it. If he caught on, he'd never want to go out with her.

And that would be the *end* of their relationship— before it even started.

[Chloe: Don't worry. He probably won't figure it out, right? I'd say the same thing, too—if I hadn't highlighted several commands and written 'use on Travis' next to them before I went to bed last

night. Sometimes being organized is not such a good thing.]

"Travis!" Chloe called. But at the same time, the bell rang, and Travis didn't hear her. Doors opened, and kids spilled out of classrooms. Before Chloe could move, Travis disappeared into the crowd, taking the book with him.

chapter
ten

"I still can't believe it," Chloe moaned to Riley in the trailer the next day. "I staked out every one of Travis's classrooms and I never saw him!"

"Maybe he cut," Riley suggested. She pulled a red top from her duffel bag and shook it out. "Is he home now?"

"His dirt bike's not there—I checked," Chloe said. "Anyway, I don't think I could actually go over and ask for the book back. I just can't face him—it would be way too embarrassing."

Chloe glanced at Riley's top. "You can't wear that to California Dream. It's completely wrinkled."

"Tell me about it." Riley tossed the red top on the couch. "What are you going to wear, anyway?"

"I'm not going," Chloe declared.

"What? How can you say that?" Riley demanded. "This is Sierra's big concert! It's a major event. Everybody's going!"

"Exactly," Chloe said. "E*verybody's* going. Everybody who witnessed my total humiliation yesterday will be there."

"But nobody will be looking at you," Riley argued. She pulled a green top from her backpack. "They're going to watch Sierra and the band, remember? Besides, everybody's forgotten about yesterday. It's old news by now."

"Ha," Chloe said. "No one forgets a disaster like that. Not overnight."

Riley shook out the green top. "This one's even more wrinkled," she said with a frown. "Does Dad have an iron? Where is he, anyway?"

"He went to buy a new deck chair," Chloe told her. "One of them collapsed under him this morning. Then he's going grocery shopping."

Riley checked the time. "I can't wait for him. Besides, he probably doesn't have an iron. All he wears these days are shorts and T-shirts. I'll have to go by the house and get something that's not wrinkled."

"Okay. Have fun at the concert," Chloe told her. "Wish Sierra luck for me."

"Come on, Chloe," Riley said. "You can't hide out forever."

"I know," Chloe admitted. "But I really need a little more time before I can face anybody—like maybe a month!"

● ● ●

A few minutes later, Riley reached her house and let herself into the living room. Her mother was pacing the floor, a cordless phone clamped to her ear.

"What?" Macy Carlson said into the phone. "Tedi, you sound a hundred percent better. Okay, ninety percent. Definitely better enough to come for a fitting tonight. The show *is* on Monday, remember?"

Catching sight of Riley, Mrs. Carlson waved a greeting. Riley waved back and headed upstairs.

In the bedroom, she changed into a clean pair of jeans and put on a blue top with cap sleeves and a scalloped neckline. She eyed the jeans and top she'd just taken off. Should she stuff them in the dirty clothes hamper?

The trailer didn't have a washer and dryer. Dad washed his clothes at a Laundromat in town. As far as Riley was concerned, that was no way to simplify your life.

She and Chloe would have to trek to the Laundromat tomorrow, she guessed. They didn't have enough clean clothes to last until after the MTV show. It would be great to bring the dirty ones here, but she and her sister had taken a stand. They couldn't cave in, not over clothes.

Deciding to pick up the dirty jeans and top on her way home, Riley left them in the bedroom and went downstairs.

As she got close to the living room, she heard her

mother's voice. "Trust me, Tedi, it's going to be stunning," Mrs. Carlson was saying. "The beads are gorgeous. And wait until you see the shoes you'll be wearing."

Riley entered the living room, waved to her mother, and walked toward the door.

"A pair of high-heeled slides, about four inches, skinny as toothpicks," Macy said into the phone.

Riley froze, her hand on the doorknob.

"And the straps are covered with rhinestones," her mother said. "I picked them up at a designer sale—they were the last pair. I had them in mind when I was designing the dress. They're absolutely perfect."

[Riley: Uh-oh. Are you thinking what I'm thinking? That I loaned the last pair of the perfect shoes to Sierra? That Sierra might accidentally break a heel or knock off some rhinestones? And that if I'm smart, I'll get those shoes back before Mom finds out, or Chloe won't have a sister anymore? Right—I figured that's what you were thinking.]

In a panic, Riley yanked open the door.

"Riley, I'm off the phone," her mother called out. "Tedi will be here in just a little while. Want to stick around and see her in the dress?"

"Love to, Mom, but I've got to go somewhere. Bye!" Riley hurried outside and raced away from the house.

Speeding toward California Dream, Riley crossed her fingers, hoping that Sierra would understand why she had to give back the shoes immediately. Of course, she'd have to do the show barefoot, but that might actually look cool.

As Riley approached the beach club, she heard the sound of a bass guitar and drums blasting into the night. Another guitar joined in, and then Sierra's voice began singing.

Riley groaned. The concert had already started. Now she'd have to wait until the band took a break.

The place was packed inside and out. Riley didn't even bother trying to find a seat. She threaded her way through the crowd on the beach to find a spot where she could at least see the action.

"Hi, Riley!" Larry emerged from a knot of other kids and grinned at her. "I was hoping I'd see you here. Hey, want to watch with me?"

"I can't. I have to check something out," Riley told him. Larry looked so disappointed, she felt a little sorry for him. "Look, I'll come back," she said. "You sit down here and wait for me, okay?"

"Great." Larry plopped down onto the sand.

Riley continued working her way around the crowd. She finally found a place at the outer edge, where she could still see the stage.

As Riley began to watch, the band went into a new number. It was fast, with a pounding rhythm and lots of movement from Sierra. She looked awesome, glittering with sequins and rhinestones. With the strobe lights flashing, she strutted from one side of the stage to the other, jumping, kicking, and whirling around.

Riley tried to enjoy it, but all she could look at were the shoes. Why did Sierra have to move around so much? Her voice was great. Couldn't she just stand there and sing?

The third number was an instrumental, but even though Sierra didn't sing, she stayed onstage and played. She didn't jump or kick, though, and Riley was relieved.

The fourth number was slow and Sierra didn't move much in that one, either. Riley started to feel panicky. She had to get those shoes!

Riley nervously checked her watch. Tedi was probably at the house now. Was Mom looking for the shoes yet?

Hurry, hurry! Riley thought as the music continued. Pick up the beat! Take a break! Something—anything! Just let me get the shoes!

Finally, the music ended. Sierra came to the edge of the stage, sparkling in a spotlight. "We'll be taking a break after this," she told the audience.

Yes! Riley thought.

"And we'll need it." Sierra grinned. "I think you'll see why. One...two...three!"

The band launched into a loud, fast number with a pounding beat. Sierra's voice soared above the wailing guitars. She was a sparkling whirlwind, spinning her way around the stage. The crowd really got into it, clapping their hands over their heads and dancing in the sand.

Riley tapped her foot and waited for the song to end. She knew this number and she loved it, but she was barely hearing it.

Just get it over with, she kept thinking. Finish the song, take a break, and give me the shoes!

The music slowed for a second. Riley knew the big windup was finally coming. It would be all over in about a minute.

With a loud crash of drums, the band lit into the final bars. Sierra pranced back and forth, tossing her long red hair, plucking low notes from her guitar. As she marched to one side of the stage and kicked out with her leg, the shoe shot off her foot.

Spinning like a sparkler, the shoe soared through the air, over the heads of the audience.

Riley gasped.

The crowd laughed and clapped.

Sierra didn't miss a beat. She whirled around and kicked in the other direction.

The second shoe went airborne.

The crowd screamed happily. They were loving it.

"Noooo!" Riley screamed in a panic. She was doomed.

chapter
eleven

"**N**oooo!" Riley screamed again. Both shoes had disappeared! This was a total nightmare! She had to get them back!

The first shoe had sailed in her direction. Spinning around to go find it, she crashed straight into Joelle and Carrie.

"Oof!" Carrie gasped. "Oh, hi, Riley."

"Hi, Riley, isn't the concert—" Carrie started to say.

"Do you see it?" Riley asked, frantically scanning the sand for anything that sparkled.

"See what?" Joelle asked.

"The shoe! It went that way!" Riley cried. As she pointed along the sand, she suddenly spotted the shoe. "There it is!" Leaving Carrie and Joelle, she pushed her way through the crowd.

Kids were milling around, talking and laughing. Some were dancing, even though the music had stopped. Riley tried to make a beeline for the shoe, but people kept getting in her way.

When Riley was about three feet from the glittering shoe, a girl who was dancing spun around and kicked it by accident.

"Oh, no!" Riley cried as the shoe tumbled farther away from her. She dropped to her knees, peering through a sea of moving legs. Yes! There it was!

"Riley, what are you doing?"

Riley quickly glanced up. "Hi, Quinn," she said to Chloe's friend. She looked back toward the shoe. Too many legs in the way again.

"Did you lose something?" Quinn asked. "And, hey, where's Chloe?"

"Hiding," Riley replied, crawling sideways in hopes of getting a better view. "Sierra's shoes."

"Huh?" Quinn sounded confused.

The crowd shifted and Riley could finally see again. But the shoe was gone.

Riley jumped up and grabbed Quinn's arm. "Did you see Sierra's shoes?" she asked in a panic.

"Yeah, when they were flying through the air," Quinn said. "What's going on?"

Riley didn't have time to explain. She dropped down again and scanned the sand. There was something sparkly! Was it the shoe? "Tell you later, Quinn," she said, and scooted around a bunch of dancers toward the shiny object.

But the shiny object turned out to be a flashlight with a silver handle.

Riley gazed around desperately. What happened to the shoe? Bumping her way through the crowd, she asked everyone she ran into if they'd seen it, but no one had.

What am I going to do? Riley wondered. Mom is absolutely going to kill me!

[**Riley: Everybody's been through this, right? You mess up and you know you're going to get caught. You imagine the entire miserable scene. First the blow-up: your mom (or dad or whoever) yells for a minute. Then she stops. But you know she's still sizzling mad because you can practically see the smoke coming out of her ears. You've already apologized and if you say anything else, it'll just set her off again. So you stand there hanging your head and waiting for the ax to fall.**]

"Hi, Riley!" Larry's voice called out from behind her. "Hey, look what I found!"

Riley turned.

Larry grinned at her…and held out the missing shoe.

"Larry! I can't believe it!" Riley cried. "This is so fantastic! Where did you find it?"

"Right behind you. You were about to step on it," he told her.

"Thanks, Larry, this is totally great!" Riley said.

"I'm going to give it back to Sierra," Larry said. "Want to come with me?"

"No! Don't give it to Sierra!" Riley cried.

"Huh?" Larry looked baffled. "It's hers, isn't it? I saw it take off when she kicked her leg."

"Right, but it's not *really* hers. See, I—" Riley stopped herself. She didn't have time to explain. She had to get that shoe.

"Larry," Riley said, looking him in the eye. "Please. Let me have the shoe."

"Okay. Sure." Larry handed it to her.

"Great!" Riley said. "Thanks, Larry." She blew the sand from the strap and checked it out. No missing rhinestones as far as she could tell. "One shoe down, one to go."

"Huh? Oh, I get it," Larry said. "You want the other shoe, right?"

"Yes!" Riley agreed enthusiastically. "Want to help me find it?"

He grinned. "Sure!"

"Okay, come on!" Riley began making her way toward the area where the other shoe had fallen. "Let's find it! Come on, boy!"

Larry loped along eagerly. There were still lots of kids milling around. Riley asked dozens of them about the shoe, but no one had seen that one, either.

When they reached the critical area, Larry crawled

through the crowd, pawing sand from every shiny object he or Riley spotted. More cans turned up, plus an empty key chain and a broken watchband.

But no second shoe.

Riley's hopes had been high at first, but they were sinking fast by the time the band returned to the stage.

She stood on tiptoe and looked at the stage. Sierra's feet were bare. No one had given the shoe back to her. Riley's last hope vanished.

"Okay, that's it." She sighed.

Larry was on his hands and knees, brushing sand away from something. It turned out to be a shiny silver hair-clip.

"Larry, stop," Riley told him.

He glanced up. "Why?"

"Because I have to go home," Riley said. She had to face the wrath of Mom.

"Well, okay. But I'll keep looking if you want," he said.

"Really? Are you sure?" Riley asked, surprised. After all, she hadn't exactly been treating him too well lately.

"I'm sure," Larry told her. "Anything you want, Riley."

"Thanks, Larry. I mean it." Riley held out the one shoe. "Don't forget what it looks like. And if you find the other one, bring it to my house, okay?"

"Got it," Larry said. He went back to his search.

Riley could hear the band playing as she started home. But after a few minutes, the music faded away. She walked along the beach and kept her eyes on the sand. Maybe someone had taken the shoe and then dropped it somewhere. Maybe she'd get lucky and see it.

And maybe Mom wouldn't ground her for the rest of her natural life.

A dog barked and Riley glanced up. Chloe and Pepper were walking toward her.

"Is the concert over already?" Chloe asked.

Riley shook her head and held up the single shoe.

"Where's the other one?" Chloe asked. "Uh-oh. What happened?"

Riley told her. "I have to go home and break the news to Mom. Be sure to bring Pepper to visit me while I'm in the dungeon." She leaned down and patted the puppy. "Hey, I just realized—she's sitting."

Chloe nodded. "She isn't tugging on the leash as much, either. I decided I might as well work harder on teaching her a few of the basics. After all, I have to do something with my life since I ruined my chances with Travis."

"Maybe they're not *totally* ruined," Riley told her.

"Just like Mom might not be mad about the shoes?" Chloe asked.

"That's different. But we can talk about it later," Riley said. "If I don't go home and confess now, I'll probably chicken out."

Chloe wished her sister luck, then continued walking with the dog.

Riley was wrong about Travis. Chloe was sure that any chance she might have had with him was gone. The worst part was, it was her own fault.

It was so embarrassing. How could she have acted that way? So superficial—smiling like an idiot, posing on the deck, staking out his locker? Trying to use dog-training commands on him and actually following him into the boys' bathroom!

Every time Chloe thought about yesterday's disaster, she wanted to drop into a hole and never come out.

Up ahead, Chloe saw the lights of California Dream and heard music and clapping. Time to go back. She still wasn't ready to face anybody.

"Come on, Pepper." She turned and tugged gently on the leash. The dog turned with her and they started back.

After a few paces, Chloe suddenly stopped. Oh, no. Was that Travis walking toward her?

Yes. Definitely. Travis Morgan was coming her way. Walking beside him on a leash was a big dog with shaggy brown fur that she'd never seen before.

Chloe picked up Pepper and glanced around, looking for a place to hide. She couldn't face Travis now. She was too embarrassed. Plus her hair was a wreck and her shorts were baggy. Not fashionably baggy, either. Stretched-out-of-shape baggy.

Travis was coming closer.

Chloe wanted to run, but she made herself stand

still. She owed Travis an apology. That was the important thing. How could she worry about her looks now? Hadn't she just decided she was too superficial?

Chloe put the dog down. She rolled the cuffs of her shorts up over her knees and twisted her hair into a knot at the back of her neck.

[Chloe: Okay, I couldn't stop myself. Major changes don't happen overnight. And not worrying about how I look is definitely a major change.]

As Travis and his dog drew close, Chloe took a deep breath and said, "Hi."

"Hi." Travis stopped. His dog sat by his feet, eyeing Pepper as if she might make a good snack. Pepper wagged her tail.

Chloe nervously cleared her throat. "I, um, I didn't know you had a dog."

"He's my uncle's. I'm just taking care of him for a few days," Travis explained. "He needs training, and this is helping."

To Chloe's horror, Travis held out the dog-training book.

"Look, Travis, about that book," she said. "I can explain—"

"Don't worry about it," he told her.

"Really?" Chloe smiled. Maybe this wouldn't be so hard after all. "I felt bad about it and I wanted to apologize. I thought you'd be mad."

"No. I admire it," Travis said. "You were just experimenting with simple behavior modification techniques to determine if behavior patterns of canines were uniform with those of high mammals."

Huh? "Yeah, right," Chloe agreed. "What you said."

"Well, see you." Travis handed the book to Chloe and began walking away.

Chloe riffled the pages of the book. "Hey, Travis?" she called.

He stopped and looked at her.

"I put my science homework in this book," Chloe told him. "You didn't happen to see it, did you?"

"See it? I ate it." Travis winked. "Woof," he said, and walked away with his dog.

chapter
twelve

Riley took a deep breath and slipped into the beach house through the kitchen door.

The kitchen was empty. Riley stood still for a moment, listening. How come it was so quiet? No music, no TV, no talking. But she'd seen Tedi's little blue roadster parked outside.

What was happening?

Could Mom possibly not have noticed that the shoes were missing yet? After all, if she had, she'd definitely be making a lot of noise looking for them.

Grabbing a paper towel, Riley carefully brushed more sand from the shoe. All the rhinestones seemed to be there. But so what? The other shoe was still lost.

For a second, Riley toyed with the idea of sneaking the shoe in and then splitting before Mom saw her. Mom would find one shoe, but the second would just never turn up. No one would be able to explain it.

Riley perked up a little. It might work. She could see it now—over the years the tale would become a family legend, passed down through the generations. As Riley wondered whether she really had the nerve to try it, a loud thumping sound came from upstairs.

Okay, there was the noise. She'd been expecting it, but she still winced.

More thumping noises from above. Then footsteps hurried toward the kitchen and Manuelo rushed in, looking frazzled.

"Hi, Manuelo," Riley said.

Manuelo gasped, startled. When he spotted the shoe, he gasped again.

"Looking for this?" Riley asked.

"Yes!" he cried. "Riley, thank goodness! Your mother is tearing the house apart trying to find those shoes!"

"I figured that's what all the thumping was about," Riley said.

Manuelo nodded. "Your mother and Tedi are upstairs going through closets. She's had me looking in the garage."

"You're kidding? The garage?"

"My reaction exactly," Manuelo said. "I wanted to ask her who keeps shoes like that in the garage, but considering her mood, it wasn't a wise question."

Riley groaned. "Don't tell me—her mood's bad, right?"

"And getting worse," Manuelo agreed. "But she's

nervous about the show. After all, it's only two days away." He smiled. "It doesn't matter now, though. You have the shoes! Where did you find them?"

"Not them. It," Riley said. She told Manuelo what had happened. So much for sneaking in and out. It wouldn't have worked, anyway. Her mother would ask her about them, naturally, and Riley wouldn't be able to lie.

Manuelo shook his head sympathetically. "What are you going to do?"

"I'm going to tell her," Riley said. She cringed as more thumping noises came from above. "Then I'm going to throw myself at her feet and beg for mercy."

Footsteps pounded down the stairs. "They have to be here!" Macy Carlson's voice declared. "If I have to rip this house apart to find them, I will!"

Riley groaned again. "This is going to be *so* hard."

Manuelo patted her shoulder. "Make it fast," he advised. "It'll be less painful that way. For both of us."

"What do you mean?"

"When the house is ripped apart, guess whose job it is to clean it up?" he reminded her. He patted her shoulder again. "Go on. Be brave and get it over with."

Clutching the shoe, Riley walked through the living room and stopped in the doorway of her mother's workroom. From the shoeboxes and shoes scattered across the floor, she could tell the room had already been searched. Her mother and Tedi were on their knees, obviously looking again.

Riley tucked the shoe behind her back and tapped on the doorframe. "Hi."

Her mother and Tedi glanced up. Macy Carlson's brown hair was tangled and her expression was frantic. Tedi's long black hair was a mess, too, and her face was flushed.

"Riley! Honey, I'm afraid I can't spend any time with you tonight after all," Mrs. Carlson said. "I'm in the middle of a crisis."

"A major crisis," Tedi agreed in a stuffy voice. Because of her cold, the word *major* came out "bajor." She sniffed loudly. "I'm a wreck, Bacy," she said to Riley's mother.

"Yes, but you'll be fine by Monday night," Macy insisted. "Your cold's much better. Keep telling yourself that. And keep looking for the shoes!"

Okay. It was time. Riley couldn't put it off any longer. She took the slide from behind her back. "I found a shoe," she announced.

Her mother's head snapped up and her eyes widened. "That's *it*!" she screamed, scrambling to her feet and taking the shoe. "Riley, what…how…where?"

"Um…" Riley said.

"Where's the other one?" Tedi asked, cutting to the chase.

Riley knew she had to answer, but she couldn't make herself do it yet. "Um…" she repeated.

"I love it," Tedi said, taking the shoe from Macy. "Too

bad I can't wear just one—because it's really beautiful."

"Riley…" Mrs. Carlson started to say.

"Wait!" Riley had a sudden inspiration. Actually, it was a totally desperate idea, but it was worth a shot. "Mom, Tedi, listen!" Riley said. "Forget about the other shoe. A girl in school—she's a junior and she always wears the coolest clothes—was walking down the hall the other day and she had only one shoe on. Then, the next day, two more girls started wearing just one shoe! Get it?"

Tedi frowned. Mrs. Carlson raised an eyebrow.

Riley babbled on. "It's a new trend! Nobody else is doing it but a few high school kids, and you know how that works," she said. "It'll catch on and pretty soon you'll start seeing it everywhere."

"It won't last," Tedi predicted.

"Maybe not," Riley admitted. "That's why now is the time to get in on it, see? Mom, you'll be the first in the fashion industry to do it! You have a chance to be totally on the cutting edge! Just think of all the people who'll see it on MTV!"

Mrs. Carlson didn't comment, but Tedi did. "It *could* happen, I guess," she said, frowning at the shoe. "But…only one shoe? How's that going to look?"

"I'll show you." Riley pulled off one of her sneakers and walked into the living room. Her mother and Tedi followed and watched as she strode back and forth in front of the couch.

"See?" Riley said as she demonstrated. "Of course, I'm not a model. You'll look much better, Tedi."

"You're limping a little," Tedi told her.

"That's what's cool about it," Riley said, trying desperately to sound convincing. "Everything cool starts out looking weird, you know. Dark brown lipstick used to look weird. So did nose rings and tattoos and, well, you get the idea, right? Go on, Tedi," Riley urged. "Try it."

Tedi stepped out of her own shoes and slid a foot into the high-heeled shoe.

"Go on, walk!" Riley told her.

Tedi began walking. The slide was much higher than a sneaker. Her bare foot thumped every time she took a step, and her head bobbed up and down.

Tedi might as well be on a pogo stick, Riley thought hopelessly. Mom's definitely not going to go for it. Bracing herself, she checked out her mother's reaction.

[**Riley**: Oh, boy. See that expression on her face? That's called suspicion. Not only is Mom not buying my stupid idea, she knows I have something to do with the missing shoe.]

"Riley, what is going on?" Mrs. Carlson demanded. "Tedi, stop hobbling around," she added. "You'll break your ankle."

Tedi sank onto the couch. "Trust me, Riley, this will never be a hot trend. It won't even get warm."

Mrs. Carlson crossed her arms. And Riley knew it

was all over. When Mom crossed her arms, she meant business.

"Okay, Riley," her mother said. "What happened to the other shoe?"

"Well, it's a long story," Riley began.

"I'm not going anywhere," her mother said.

"Sure, I knew that. I was just figuring out where to start." Riley breathed deeply. "Okay, it's like this…" she said.

chapter
thirteen

Before Riley could say any more, a door slammed, a dog yipped, and Chloe rushed into the living room with Pepper at her side.

"Chloe, please!" Mrs. Carlson cried. "Take that dog out of here before it waters the rug again and drives me completely over the edge!"

"Pepper won't do anything," Chloe assured her. "We've been walking for an hour and she's empty, take my word for it."

"Dogs are never empty, especially puppies," Macy declared. "I told you—"

"Mom, please," Chloe interrupted. She pushed on the puppy's rear end and got it to sit. "Listen, the most incredible thing happened. You'll never believe it. Guess."

Riley jumped in quickly to keep their mother from freaking. "Hey, Chloe? This is not a good time for a guessing game."

"Oh, all right." Chloe paused. "At least close your eyes."

"Chloe!" Riley said.

"Okay, okay, I won't torture you." With a grin, Chloe reached into the pouch of her sweatshirt and pulled out the missing shoe. "Ta-da!"

Riley's mouth dropped open.

Mrs. Carlson shrieked.

Tedi laughed and held up the first shoe. "It's a match!"

"Chloe, you've saved the day!" her mother cried.

"And my life!" Riley added excitedly. She hugged her sister, then collapsed into a chair with a big sigh of relief. She might still be in trouble for taking the shoes in the first place, but it couldn't be as bad.

"Where did you find it?" Tedi asked.

"I didn't," Chloe said.

"Did Larry find it?" Riley asked. "He said he'd keep looking for it."

Chloe shook her head no. Still grinning, she pointed to the puppy, who had scooted under the coffee table. "Pepper found it!"

"The *dog*? No!" Macy said.

"Yes!" Chloe cried. "I was walking her on the beach after I ran into Travis—don't ask me about that yet—and I decided to let her run off the leash for a minute. All of a sudden, she started digging in the sand. I called her and she came running back with the shoe in her mouth."

"What a great dog!" Riley pulled the puppy from under the coffee table and kissed her between the eyes. "You saved me, Pepper! What a good, smart dog you are!"

"What I want to know is, how did the shoe get on the beach in the first place?" Macy asked.

"Good question," Tedi agreed.

"Okay, confession time," Riley said, and explained the whole story. "I know I shouldn't have taken them," she admitted. "I'm really sorry, Mom."

Her mother looked exasperated. "Honestly, Riley."

"Really, really sorry," Riley said.

"Well, at least they're back," Tedi said. She took the second shoe from Chloe and checked it out. "I think it survived, Macy. Except for a little dog drool and sand."

Mrs. Carlson took some tissues and wiped the shoe clean. Tedi slipped both of them on and walked around the living room. "Two are definitely better than one, Riley."

Riley laughed. "I was desperate."

"So was I," her mother said. "I thought the shoes were gone for good. Isn't it amazing how things can change in an instant?" She bent down and scratched Pepper between the ears. "And it's all because of you, isn't it, sweetie?"

Pepper wagged her tail.

"Yes, you're such a good dog," Mrs. Carlson crooned. "A very good dog. As soon as the show's over,

I'm going to buy you a whole box of puppy biscuits."

[Riley: Whoa! Do you hear the way she's talking to Pepper? Is it possible she's softening up? Maybe we just got Pepper at a bad time.]

"You mean we can keep Pepper?" Riley asked.

"Here at the house?" Chloe added.

"That's what I mean," their mother said, giving the dog one last pat. "Now. Tedi and I are going to do a fitting, so take your dog out of here, please. I like her, but I still don't trust her."

"Thanks for letting us stay here, Dad," Chloe said at the trailer the next day. "It was great of you."

"Really," Riley agreed.

"Hey, I loved having you here," Jake told them. "I'm just glad things worked out with the puppy and your mom."

"And now you'll be able to use all the hot water you want," Riley joked.

Their father laughed. "So will you." He held out his arms, and Riley and Chloe gave him a big hug. Then they picked up their bags and left the trailer.

As they walked away, Riley noticed something. "You're not checking to see if Travis is around," she said.

Chloe nodded. "After what he said at the beach last night, I decided I might as well give up."

"No way. I don't believe it," Riley said.

"It's true," Chloe told her. After they'd walked for a few minutes, she said, "Okay, maybe you're right. I'm not giving up."

"I knew it."

"But I *am* going to give it a rest," Chloe declared.

"Good idea," Riley agreed. "Make him wonder why you're all of a sudden ignoring him. Hang out with other boys. Let him see what he's missing."

"Exactly." Chloe grinned. "You're catching on, Riley. I knew you would."

Riley laughed. "Gee, thanks."

Chloe suddenly stopped walking and pointed down the beach. "Hey, is that Larry out there in front of California Dream?"

Riley shaded her eyes and peered down the beach. California Dream wasn't open yet. The only person around was kneeling in the sand behind it. Kneeling…and digging.

"It *is* Larry," Riley said. "He said he'd keep looking for the other shoe. But he couldn't have stayed out there all night!"

"Well, this *is* Larry we're talking about," Chloe reminded her.

"You're right!" Feeling guilty, Riley hunched her bags up and trotted down the beach. "Larry!" she called out. "Hey, Larry!"

Larry raised his head. "Hi, Riley. Listen, I hate to tell you, but I think that shoe is gone for good."

"It's okay, Pepper found it," Riley told him. "Larry, I feel awful. I mean, I never thought you'd look for it all night."

"I'd do anything for you, Riley," Larry said.

"Oh, no!" Riley felt terrible.

"Anything except maybe stay out all night digging for a shoe," Larry added. "I came back this morning."

"Oh, good!" Riley sighed with relief. "That was really nice of you, Larry, but you can stop now."

"Right." Larry squinted up at them. "What's the deal with the bags? Are you two going on some kind of trip or something?"

"Sort of," Chloe said.

"It's a long story," Riley added. She hesitated. "Why don't you walk home with us and we'll tell you all about it?" she asked.

Chloe glanced at her in surprise.

"Sure!" Larry jumped up eagerly. "I left a bottle of water on the deck. Just let me get it."

As Larry dashed toward the deck, Chloe nudged Riley in the arm. "Why did you ask him to come with us? I mean, you're always trying to get rid of him."

"Yeah. But he was trying to help," Riley explained. "It wouldn't be fair to just give him a pat on the head and say 'Good boy.' Like I said, boys are human beings."

"You're right," Chloe agreed. Then she grinned. "I guess I finally figured that out—if you want to train a boy, don't treat him like a dog!"

Chloe
and Riley's

SCRAPBOOK

WIN
a trip to the set and meet Mary-Kate and Ashley sweepstakes

  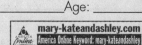

SO LITTLE TIME™

Win a Trip to the Set and Meet Mary-Kate and Ashley Sweepstakes

OFFICIAL RULES:

1. No purchase necessary.

2. To enter complete the official entry form or hand print your name, address, and phone number along with the words "*So Little Time* Trip to the Set Sweepstakes" on a 3 x 5 card and mail to: *So Little Time* Trip to the Set Sweepstakes, c/o HarperEntertainment, Attn: Children's Marketing Department, 10 E 53rd Street, New York, NY, 10022. Entries must be received no later than September 2nd, 2002. Enter as often as you wish, but each entry must be mailed separately. One entry per envelope. Partially completed, illegible or mechanically reproduced entries will not be accepted. Sponsors are not responsible for lost, late, mutilated, illegible, stolen, postage due, incomplete or misdirected entries. All entries become the property of HarperCollins Publishers, Inc. ("HarperCollins"), and will not be returned.

3. Sweepstakes open to all legal residents of the United States (excluding Colorado and Rhode Island), who are between the ages of five and fifteen by September 2nd, 2002, excluding employees and immediate family members of HarperCollins, Parachute Properties and Parachute Press, Inc., and their respective subsidiaries and affiliates, officers, directors, shareholders, employees, agents, attorneys, and other representatives (individually and collectively "Parachute"), Dualstar Entertainment Group, Inc., and its subsidiaries and affiliates, officers, directors, shareholders, employees, agents, attorneys, and other representatives (individually and collectively "Dualstar"), and their respective parent companies, affiliates, subsidiaries, advertising, promotion and fulfillment agencies, and the persons with whom each of the above are domiciled. Offer void where prohibited or restricted by law.

4. Odds of winning depend on the total number of entries received. Approximately 75,000 sweepstakes notifications published. All prizes will be awarded. Winners will be randomly drawn on or about September 16th, 2002, by HarperCollins, whose decisions are final. Potential winners will be notified by mail and will be required to sign and return an affidavit of eligibility and release of liability within 14 days of notification. Prizes won by minors will be awarded to parent or legal guardian who must sign and return all required legal documents. By acceptance of their prize, winners consent to the use of their names, photographs, likeness, and personal information by HarperCollins, Parachute, and Dualstar, and for publicity purposes without further compensation except where prohibited.

5. One (1) Grand Prize Winner will receive a visit to the *So Little Time* set, or other Mary-Kate and Ashley production, where they will meet Mary-Kate and Ashley Olsen. HarperCollins, Parachute, and Dualstar, reserve the right to substitute another prize of equal or of greater value in the event that the winner is unable to receive the prize for any reason.

   HarperEntertainment will provide the contest winner and one parent or legal guardian, with round-trip air transportation from major airport nearest winner to Los Angeles, standard hotel accommodations for a two-night stay, a visit to the set of *So Little Time*, or other Mary-Kate and Ashley production, $500 spending money, and the chance to meet Mary-Kate and Ashley Olsen, subject to availability. Approximate retail value of prize: $3000. Trip must be taken within one year from the date prize is awarded, or the prize will be forfeited, and may be subject to blackout dates. All additional expenses including taxes, meals, gratuities, and incidentals are the responsibility of the prize winner. Airline, accommodation and other travel arrangements will be made by HarperCollins in its discretion. Travel and use of accommodation are at risk of winner and HarperCollins does not assume any liability.

6. Only one prize will be awarded per individual, family, or household. Prizes are non-transferable and cannot be sold or redeemed for cash. No cash substitute is available except at HarperCollins's sole discretion. Any federal, state, or local taxes are the responsibility of the winner. Sponsor may substitute prize of equal or greater value, if necessary, due to availability.

7. *Additional terms:* By participating, entrants agree a) to the official rules and decisions of the judges, which will be final in all respects; and to waive any claim to ambiguity of the official rules and b) to release, discharge, and hold harmless HarperCollins, Parachute, Dualstar, and their affiliates, subsidiaries, and advertising and promotion agencies from and against any and all liability or damages associated with acceptance, use, or misuse of any prize received in this sweepstakes.

8. Any dispute arising from this Sweepstakes will be determined according to the laws of the State of New York, without reference to its conflict of law principles, and the entrants consent to the personal jurisdiction of the State and Federal courts located in New York County and agree that such courts have exclusive jurisdiction over all such disputes.

9. To obtain the name of the winners, please send your request and a self-addressed stamped envelope (not required for residents of Vermont and Washington) to *So Little Time* Trip to the Set Sweepstakes, c/o HarperEntertainment, 10 East 53rd Street, New York, NY 10022 by October 1st, 2002. Sweepstakes sponsor: HarperCollins Publishers, Inc.

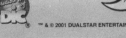

3 NEW VIDEOS FROM MARY-KATE & ASHLEY!

mary–kateandashley TRAVELINSTYLE™ GIFTSET

Comes packed with LOTS of stuff to travel from sun to snow!

Fashionable looks for snowboarding and ice skating!

Trendiest suits for bodyboarding or just hanging out!

FREE BOOK INCLUDED